MYS
Lov

Lovell, Marc

Good spies dont grow on trees.

Good Spies Don't
Grow on Trees

By Marc Lovell

Good Spies Don't Grow on Trees

MARC LOVELL

PUBLISHED FOR THE CRIME CLUB BY
DOUBLEDAY & COMPANY, INC.
GARDEN CITY, NEW YORK
1986

All of the characters in this book
are fictitious, and any resemblance
to actual persons, living or dead,
is purely coincidental.

Library of Congress Cataloging-in-Publication Data

Lovell, Marc.
Good spies don't grow on trees.

I. Title.
PR6062.0853G6   1986   823'.914   86-11548
ISBN 0-385-23836-3

Good Spies Don't
Grow on Trees

ONE

Apple was brought gently awake by the coldness of his feet. Being six feet seven inches from the roots of his fair hair, they often suffered that way at night, especially here at the cottage, where his bed was shorter than in the Bloomsbury apartment. If it weren't for his secret dread of dying while asleep, to be found by some stranger, who might snigger, Apple would have worn bedsocks.

He yawned. This drove away the last vestige of sleep, forcing him to get active, bring his arms out from under the covers. One hand was for covering the taut, gaping mouth, the other for dithering in the air nearby.

The face Apple next gave a good rub to was pale. Its features were average, its style had a hint of the timid, its freckles were like speckles from a brush doing orange. The green eyes said to forget that timidity—if you didn't mind them mentioning it.

Reaching out a long yet substantial arm, Appleton Porter pulled the plug on his electric alarm clock. He smiled a show smile in self-congratulation: rather than be shocked awake by the awful grind of the bell, as frightening as a sick child, he had cleverly managed to wake himself up first.

After rubbing his feet together while loaning all his attention to the outdoors bird-song, Apple got out of bed. He went to the crouch-in closet. There he put on his robe, a shriek and stammer of red stripes and black blobs. He crossed uprightly under raised beams to the window, which he uncurtained and swung open to breathe in the icy clamminess of a typical English spring morning.

All around lay tree-dotted countryside, with the nearest rooftop a toy. A third-class road sauntered past in front of the garden, winding off into trees as if to emphasise the cottage's isolation. Apple had long considered his weekend home ideal for that dangerous/romantic rendezvous that might never take place.

At a bark, one bark, Apple looked below to the dog on his patch of scurvy lawn. Monico, an Ibizan hound, a gingery look-alike for the taller type of whippet, gazed back up with poignant accusation.

"Be right down," Apple said, nodding. To make sure, he jabbed a forefinger downwards.

Seconds later he was letting Monico into his parlour. The room, Apple knew, was as stagy as a coach with its horse-brasses on the beams, its chintz and warming pans and guffaw fireplace. But he was relieved to have decided that it would be unfair to his late aunt, who had willed him the cottage, if he were to alter the decor, which he liked. As a gesture of independence, he never cleaned the brassware.

Monico arrived first in the kitchen, where he waited panting until he got his Monday-morning special, corn flakes. He ate noisily, whereas Apple was silent with his porridge. This had nothing to do with the food's flaccid nature. He was thinking morosely about his latest ex-girl-friend, the ex having been added Sunday at breakfast after an argument over politics. Apple was inclined to become loud and irate on the subject, mainly because to his own ears he always sounded wrong.

Stopping himself before going into yet another replay of his own version of the argument, with the ex again coming off worst, Apple spooned like a hungry lover. Finished, he got up and bustled. He didn't want to be late. He had never been late for work in his life.

Appleton Porter, who spoke seven foreign languages with perfection, plus a dozen or so more with smooth skill, was a senior official at the United Kingdom Philological Institute, which had its home in a Kensington mansion. No one there knew of his other job.

Since leaving university, Apple had been attached to a department of British Intelligence. Officially known by a series of numbers, unofficially called Upstairs, it often made use of Apple's gift for languages. He served both as a translator of the classified and as an interpreter at meetings of Western secret services when they were pretending to be honest with each other.

Otherwise, Apple had seldom been used as an espionage operative, an agent in the field. To his sorrow, his Control from Upstairs, Angus Watkin, seemed to consider him less than ideal as a spy. It wasn't simply that he stood an unhideable seventy-nine inches tall. There were other drawbacks.

Apple finished the dishes and went upstairs. Showered, he changed into everyday clothes. In contrast to his robe, and to its Bloomsbury colleague in vicious foot-square tartan, his suit was darkly drab, like a backward bard. Furthermore, the tie matched. Apple would have sighed at himself in the mirror if he hadn't already done so a thousand times.

Leaving by the kitchen door, he set off over fields, heading for the farm where his dog lodged during the week. It didn't bother him that Monico bounded ahead and then made a fuss of Farmer Galling, before walking off without a farewell like a released convict. They went through this every Monday.

In his jovial stance, shoulders back, Apple asked, "Will we have some rain today?"

"Not a drop."

"That'll be nice."

"Nice?" Farmer Galling said slowly, as though he had been told that's what taxes were. He was a red-cheeked, burly man in tweeds the colour of manure. "Nice?"

The tedious weather-abuse that followed from Galling was another regular Monday morning feature. Apple stood it politely. By glaring slightly he managed to keep his eyes from taking on a glaze. Only when time had become severely limited did he back off with an apology.

Now, he thought in turning away, leaving Galling still at it, he would have to hustle, maybe break the law, and even then he might not get to the Institute in time. It was going to be touch and go.

Wondering absently why he always made that stupid mistake of mentioning the weather to Galling, Apple jogged back to the cottage. He collected his overnight bag, plus two video films (a recent Stallone, an old Attenborough), which he would swap with others for next weekend, locked up and strode to the side parking area. He got swiftly into Ethel.

The response was instant. Within seconds Apple was spraying gravel behind him as he shot out onto the road. He settled to driving, his face as grim as Ethel's was bright.

The vehicle, older than her owner by several years, was a retired London taxi. Nothing had been changed except the secret occupation and the colour: service with various espionage agencies had become private life, traditional black had turned to pale green, orange and red. If Ethel had such a thing as a regret, Apple felt, it was not in respect of her change of raiment.

The narrow byways were as straight as a drunk's amble, which failed to curb Apple's speed. All he needed now, he fumed, was to get stuck behind a hay cart. The fact that he hadn't seen a hay cart in years he ignored.

Presently Ethel was entering London's outer suburbs, those squashed monuments to the British gift for lack of originality. Traffic was heavier and Apple was grimmer.

Ahead, a man stepped into the roadway. He was middle-aged, white-haired, pinch-faced and small, wore a blue boiler suit and dirty white running shoes. He stopped and put his thumb out: the classic hitcher.

Apple, who never gave lifts, except to females, age immaterial, put his foot on the brake and steered into the side.

"Thought you'd never show up," Albert said as Ethel drew level. His accent was as Cockney as bows on a Limehouse belle, his tone was offended.

"Is that so?" Apple asked, chill despite his tingle of excitement. He didn't know that it wasn't Albert himself whom he disliked, but the fact that, as Angus Watkin's batman-assistant, he ought to have been a suave, silent shadow, not a crumpled gnome with a crass sense of humour.

Albert said, "When you going to get a telephone in that jungle dump of yours?"

"Are you conducting a census?"

"Now now, don't take that altitude."

While the older man snorted a laugh at the joke he had used several dozen times, Apple sighed. He said, "When you've run out of merry quips and jolly wheezes, I suppose you'll tell me what you're doing here."

"I was on me way to your jungle when the bleeding car broke down."

Loving the first while hating the last, being disinterested in the mundane details of reality, Apple said, "Get in, please, and state your destination."

"I'll show you the way," Albert said. He entered the back and sat on the pull-down seat behind the driver and slid open the glass panel.

Apple, being tough with his tingle of excitement, asked as he took Ethel forwards, "Am I going to drop you off somewhere?"

"I told you I was on me way to see you."

"Ah, so you did. If not in so many words."

"Don't be cheeky," Albert said, cheerful as an urchin at the watchman's fire.

"And why did you want to see me?"

"There's someone waiting to have a word with you."

A someone who could only be Angus Watkin, Apple knew. He let his tingle have its head, run about with glee while he drove as erratically as a bat's dance. Settling again, dropping an assuring pat on the dashboard, he warned himself not to get too optimistic. Unbridled, his mind was liable to build up to a caper glamourous and exciting, set in one of the world's more exotic corners, thus rendering the reasonable a disappointment.

Therefore Apple didn't imagine Angus Watkin snapping into a telephone, "We have an emergency. In Bali. Only one man can pull this off. Get me Appleton Porter." He thought of being sent to post a letter in Leeds.

Even so, Apple permitted himself to muse that this was an odd, sudden way for his Control to make contact. Surely Watkin could have waited until his underling arrived at work, where there was a telephone in his office.

"Um—what's it all about?" Apple asked over his shoulder despite knowing he probably wouldn't get a satisfying answer—if only because it wasn't likely that Albert had one. Few were privy to the convoluted workings of Angus Watkin's mind.

Albert said poshly, "One is not at liberty to say."

"Which means you haven't a clue."

"No more questions and no more of your cheek," Albert said. "Otherwise I'll have to try to remember what that nickname of yours is."

Apple began to blush. It wasn't for himself, on account of the fact that, as a blusher of considerable standing, he was sometimes referred to as Russet. He blushed for Albert; his crudeness in hitting low, his lack of sensitivity in not realising how cruel the social affliction could be.

The attack of heat being only a grade two, Apple let it thrive instead of fighting back with his new short-term cure. Usage weakened the effect of these methods which Apple usually acquired through newspaper advertisements.

His Eastern Highness Prince Khan the Sage's remedy, the latest, was based like all the others on the concept of inner heat killing that on the surface, while that in the mind would be dealt with by the imagined scene which caused the inner heat.

You had to picture yourself in the desert, said Prince Khan the Sage in his letter from Manchester. The temperature was a hundred and thirty, and you had half a minute in which to struggle free of the tent that had collapsed on you in order to catch the helicopter which was in danger of leaving without you, and if it did, you would certainly die out there all alone without food and water.

Upstairs knew about Apple's affliction, he was aware, just as they knew of all his other drawbacks, those blocks that stood in his way in the spy game. His dossier left nothing out.

Porter, Appleton, had a sympathetic nature. He was kind to the old and the weak, had a dangerous habit of being able to see the other person's point, in spite of his age (thirty) fell in love at the first sight of tenderness. So it would be difficult for him to produce cold force when such was inevitably called for, while compassion could water down his devotion to duty on many levels.

Porter, Appleton, had a romantic view of espionage, not the desired sardonic one. His tolerance for alcohol being low, he could soon be put at a disadvantage. He had been less than brilliant on those rare occasions when, because of his languages or top-rated loyalty, he had been sent out on a mission.

Porter, Appleton, had earned the lowest training scores of his group, with a bruised six in Unarmed Combat, a winceful five in Resistance to Pain, a dubious six for Lying Ability and a whispered four in Interest in Gossip. The fact that he hadn't tried to fake his scores had earned him a zero in Guile.

Porter, Appleton, Upstairs knew and Apple avoided thinking about, was not a pro.

Albert moved to a tycoon sprawl on the full seat. He gazed out happily at the passing drabness as if it lined a yellow brick road.

Apple's blush having died of old age, he sought to relax by not thinking ahead chicken-countingly. It made him tense. A cigarette, he decided, was called for, despite his rule against smoking at the wheel. Your pleasures came first.

Apple was always kind to himself. Which embarrassed him whenever he nearly thought of it, his little pamperings and treats. He didn't know that on an obscure level of his subconscious he had long ago come to the realisation that those who were good to themselves tended to be good to others, whereas the stoics and ascetics, all unaware, were apt to keep as far from altruism as from a pariah with bad breath. Kindness, like charity, begins at home.

Apple had put out his cigarette when, abruptly, Albert said, "Next turning left, third right, fourth right, first left, stop at number sixteen."

Caught off guard, Apple scrambled around on a mental antic to retain the sequence correctly. Not for the loss of several inches in height would he have asked for a repeat.

With a casual nod he said, in relieved truth, "Got it." Glancing in his rear-view mirror, he was gladdened further to see Albert's face take on a sag of disgust. That, in turn, was increased when Apple added, "By the way, my nickname's Russet." Appleton Porter was not without courage.

The last in the series of corners took them into a street of terrace houses. The gardens had enough space to graze kittens. Soiled white collar was the sociological essence. Here might live failed policemen, retired smut peddlars and actors who had set records in resting. Few of the neighbours would know each other.

Number sixteen was as much a platitude as the rest. With Ethel locked, Apple followed Albert to the door, which opened at a push. They went inside, into a narrow hall and a smell of fried onions. From the end doorway floated a voice saying "Come in, Porter."

Angus Watkin, like the living room in which he sat, like the house itself, was a star performer at being nondescript. Middle-aged, medium in build and colouring, he had average features, plain clothes and no suggestion of unusual intellectual powers. Altogether, spymaster Watkin looked as mysterious as a stale sandwich.

"Sit down, Porter," he said in his dull voice. "I do hope I haven't interfered too greatly with your daily routine."

Apple took the matching armchair in pseudo-leather. "Anything goes in a time of crisis, sir," he said, hoping.

Glancing around the room: "Crisis?"

"I thought, you know, that this early call meant there was an emergency."

"Emergencies rarely arise," Angus Watkin said. "The early call is because you're replacing."

Apple sighed—down his nose so it wouldn't show. As a form of consolation he lied to himself that he had known perfectly well right from the start that he wasn't going to be given a real caper.

Replacing meant that you stood in for a sick operative who had been slated for a peripheral rôle: waiting around to see what time the bedroom light goes out; creating a momentary diversion; acting as one of the crowd in a set-up scene; letting somebody knock you down into a puddle of water so that somebody else can rush to your aid, which will make him appear decent to a third somebody.

Angus Watkin said, "When you're quite ready, Porter."

"I'm ready, sir."

"Tell me what, if anything, you know about a lady called Alicia Suvov."

For the second time this morning Apple sent his mind on a scurry. He found and gave "She's a chess player, sir. The only top-level female player in the world."

"Correct. Do continue."

"And she'll be coming here to London next week for a big chess deal, a tournament."

"The lady arrives today," Angus Watkin said. "Go on."

"I think that's all I know," Apple said, smiling faintly as though he did know more but wasn't prepared to say because you never knew who might be listening.

"Did you mention the lady's nationality?"

"Yes, sir," Apple phonied. "Russian."

"Quite so, Porter."

"All the best chess players are Russian."

Watkin asked a quiet, lethal "Really?"

It would have been a simple enough matter for Apple to correct his statement smoothly, to tack on "According to the Reds." But he knew the slippery ropes with Angus

Watkin, who liked to rouse confusion in his underlings as much as he liked sowing it among his enemies.

Apple coughed and mumbled his way through. "So I've heard. In a way. I mean. After all. I wouldn't know myself. I don't play chess."

"You should, Porter. It might make you a little more devious." The way Watkin pronounced the penultimate word showed that he was fully aware of Apple's ploy, and that it had been produced by a trap in the first place.

"As a matter of fact, Porter, I don't play chess either. Can't stand the game."

Out-handled on the slippery ropes, Apple said a humble "Yes, sir."

Although there was no real change in Angus Watkin's mien, he now gave the impression somehow of being a shade more at his ease. He said, "But to the nub of this matter—the estimable Alicia Suvov. She's well known around the world, of course, but in Russia her name's a household word. She's adored by the masses. At the age of twenty-eight, she has the country even more at her feet than she had when she was a prodigy."

Effacingly Apple put in, "That's why she's allowed to travel so freely abroad. She'd be a fool to want to stay this side of the Curtain."

Watkin nodded. "Defection has never been suggested in her case, for any reason, including romantic. She's a Party member from a Party family, an ardent Communist, and has never had a friend in the West."

"A true-blue Red."

"Furthermore, she has never had a lover anywhere."

"At twenty-eight, sir?"

"The Union of Soviet Socialist Republics, Porter, has a somewhat different moral code from the one we have over here. And Alicia Suvov is a stout defender of that ethic.

Sex before marriage, adultery and so forth, she considers
to be insults to the Marxist ideal."

Without thinking of present company, Apple said,
"And she probably looks like a horse."

Angus Watkin gave one cool blink. "The young lady is
acceptably pretty, I am informed by judges in these matters," he said. "To her fellow Russians, no witticism intended, she is a raging beauty."

Although seeing no wit, Apple smiled with the right
half of his mouth to be on the safe side. "Naturally, sir."

"In fact, Alicia Suvov is one of the Soviet Union's greatest propaganda assets. She's not as newsworthy and celebrated over here as they like to believe, due to the fact that
she avoids pressmen, never gives interviews and is generally unapproachable. But Icy Alice, as the tabloids have
been known to call her, is indeed an asset."

"Also," Apple said, "she doesn't cost the Kremlin a
penny. Not like space travel, etcetera." He waved his
hand, couldn't think of any etceteras, ended, "You know."

As though there had been no interruption, his Control
went on, "It would, of course, spoil the whole effect if it
were seen that Miss Suvov had watchdogs, needed to be
kept under surveillance by the KGB. Even a man acting as
a personal bodyguard, not an unusual fixture with celebri-
ties of any nationality, could tend to sour the image. So
she's free in all ways."

"She travels completely alone, sir?"

"No. There's a woman. A combination maid-masseuse-
chum. Believed not to be connected to the KGB, and if she
is, it won't be to Miss Suvov's knowledge. She views all
the secret services with distaste."

Apple almost gave his Control a shrug of sympathy.
Angus Watkin said, "The point of my preamble, Porter, is
to let you know what's in your favour and what isn't."

"I see, sir," Apple said, lying.

"Which brings us to the precise nature of your job, to be accomplished at any time over the next two days."

Keenly, eyes alert: "Yes, sir?"

"You, Porter, must be seen publicly in conversation with Alicia Suvov."

"In Russian, of course."

"No. You will speak English. Miss Suvov speaks it as perfectly as she does French and German. Your Russian, which she might find suspicious as an afterthought, you should use only as a last resort, to try to keep her talking."

"How long is this conversation to go on, sir?"

"Fifteen minutes," Angus Watkin said. "Nothing less than that. Make your approach, hold the lady's attention for the right length of time, ease gracefully away."

"I see," Apple said slowly, in truth. What he saw wasn't the nature of the caper but the difficulties in trying to engage the interest of a media-shy, unsociable person of renown who no doubt was constantly being pestered by lion-hunters, chess addicts and reporters.

With what might have been a tinge of hope in his voice, Angus Watkin asked, "We're not intimidated, are we, Porter?"

Quickly, Apple said, "Not at all, sir."

"It's in your favour that she likes tall men."

"Thank you, sir."

Watkin said, "The approach to the lady is your affair. All I require is that you talk with her in a public, peopled place during the next forty-eight hours."

Smiling as if at the absurd, Apple asked, "What, sir, if the lady won't even say hello to me?"

"That is entirely possible," Angus Watkin said. He gave the impression of having more respect for the subject than for his underling.

"What would happen then?"

"Nothing too terrible. I dare say everyone concerned

would survive. Your job is a piece of window-dressing for something else altogether."

All of which, given as blandly as any Watkin pronouncement, while still telling nothing of the mission's nature, did tell that failure in it could keep Apple for ever at the foot of the way to Upstairs.

He said, "The odds aren't in my favour, obviously, but I'll do my very best, sir."

Ignoring that, Angus Watkin reached down on the inside of the chair's arm, like a child looking for coins when the guest has gone. The buff envelope he brought up he passed over with:

"Data on Miss Suvov. Photograph, in case you haven't seen her enough in the media. Fads and hobbies and viewpoints, so you'll know verbal course to steer. Name and address of the apartment-hotel into which she'll be checking later on this morning."

Hoping he appeared sharp and spy-like, Apple said crisply, tapping the envelope on his knee, "And then I suppose I'd best destroy the info, sir."

"You may if you wish, Porter," Angus Watkin said. "Though it wouldn't really matter if you left it on your doorstep. The information comes to us by courtesy of the Alicia Suvov Fan Club, in Hampstead."

From the safe house Apple drove across London to Bloomsbury. His flat there was old and complacent, roomy and high of ceiling. It greeted him with the chill a lonely weekend creates.

The first thing Apple did, after switching on an electric fire, was telephone the United Kingdom Philological Institute to tell them of this stupid spring cold he had caught. He grumbled that it would keep him in bed for two or three days.

Next he called Viscount Tower, the apartment-hotel in

Little Venice. Miss Suvov, he heard, was due to check into her self-service flat at noon, the information given as gladly as a knife to a maniac.

While changing into something less of an office nine-to-five, Apple considered what was connected to his caper snippet, the window-dressing that might or might not get displayed, depending on the leniency of the lady.

Could be, he mused, it was not a caper at all. Wily Watkin perhaps simply wanted from his underling an un-influenced opinion on the lady's accent; or to see if he could bring this off and so could be used on something similar, and genuine; or to evaluate the chess star's response to overtures from a stranger.

If part of a real caper this was, Apple thought on, could be it was connected with the coming chess tournament, when Alicia Suvov was due to play a dozen opponents at once, as well as individual games with British masters; or she needed to be discredited for some reason and so it would be circulated in spooksville that she had been seen talking to a man from one of the Intelligence services (photos available), which would mean blowing the under-ling's cover, which the odious Watkin would happily do if it served his purpose; or this was part of a chain, wherein a series of seemingly unrelated, seemingly harmless events lead to the needed conclusion.

Apple decided not to pursue it further, but to stick with his original idea for the forestalling of disappointment: the Russian woman would slip him a letter and ask him to post it in Leeds.

Wearing jeans and a windcheater, Apple sat down to go through the envelope on Alicia Suvov. Her photograph showed a long, strong face with penetrating eyes and a no-nonsense smile, wavy brown hair long enough to touch the shoulders, overall a decided suggestion of authority.

Statistics on the reverse side gave her height as five feet nine.

Nodding approval of that, and not too cowed by the face, Apple began to read. The chess star's background he skipped over as being irrelevant, the view of her personality he chose to ignore because, having been compiled by a fan, it would be useless. That brought him to fads and fancies.

Alicia disliked a great many things, most of which, it seemed she claimed, didn't exist in Russia: violence, a lot of television, large supermarkets, political corruption, laziness, lost luggage at airports, prostitutes and train crashes.

Her likes, Apple saw at once, were in fields of which he knew little or nothing: Polish cuisine, fencing, flower arranging, committee work, Swiss literature.

It was too late to start cramming on any of these subjects, Apple knew. There wasn't time enough. He would have to find something else to use in order to dissolve the lady's outer defences.

Browsing back through her biography and the personality boost giving him no ideas, Apple realised that he would have to come up with one himself. With help.

To show how much faith he had in his brain food, Apple whistled as shrilly as a coward in the dark while going to the kitchen, putting the kettle on for tea and setting about preparing toast.

With four slices and a teapot he sat at the table. He didn't rush. On each slice he lavished butter and lemon-flavoured marmalade. Toast was good, butter was good and tea was good, but the paramount ingredient of the mystic snack, Apple knew, was that marmalade born of lemons.

Apple had tried the orange type, as well as various curds, preserves and jellies. Nothing. Not one single door of perception had creaked even ajar. The lemon it was. Infallible.

Crunching steadily between sips of tea, Apple worked through his favourite repast. Slice followed slice. His jaw movements became slower and his eyes took on a pinkness of regret as he finished slice three with still no notion of what he could use as a grabber with Alicia Suvov.

Perhaps, Apple thought, he was too worried about failing at this insignificant task to be able to concentrate properly. It wasn't the snack's fault. What he needed was to relax with his feet up, give the food a fair chance.

Apple moved to sit on the floor with the last piece of toast in hand. He lay on his back, raised his legs. Remembering in time that shoes on tables were unlucky, like hats on beds, he made do with the lower level of the chair for his feet.

He began to eat slice four. At once he felt the difference. Marmalade oozed onto his top lip and his throat felt strange. He realised that, of course, the snack was telling him this wasn't the time for finding his grabber: it would come to him the closer he got to the moment of contact at Little Venice.

Apple got up quickly, coughing and bright. He had known that his snack wouldn't fail him, he mused while putting slice four in the fridge for later, and while clearing away, and while washing off stickiness at the sink.

Before he left the flat, Apple took the Suvov documents into the bathroom, where he carefully burned them and then flushed the remaining brittle blackness down the lavatory. It felt nice.

Little Venice, in a corner of Paddington, resembles that other, bigger Venice the way three tall buildings resemble New York. But diligent searchers can, true, find glimpses of the Grand Union Canal here and there.

Viscount Tower, recently opened, was a multi-storey block in glass and steel. It resembled nothing so much as a stockpile of the latest in see-through coffins.

Apple approached on foot, having needed to leave Ethel at a distance. Cars were double-parked on the busy commercial street fronting Viscount Tower and clogged its forecourt. There were equal numbers of people coming and going and standing around. Apple strolled inside.

The lobby, expansive as the smile of a wheedling child, had white leather lounging furniture centrally, with the sides taken up by reception, entrance doors, stairs and lifts, open coffee shop. There were people everywhere.

After a scan about, forcing his eyes to be round, not crafty, Apple went over to the coffee shop area. He sat on one of the swivel-stools, swung completely around three times, ordered an orange juice. While being served, he asked if there was anything new on Alicia Suvov. The waitress said, "Who?"

Swinging back midway, sipping his drink, Apple had a more thorough look at all those present. He felt it quite possible that the Russian chess star, despite what Angus Watkin had said, would have some sort of protector watching unobtrusively from the sidelines.

Among the sitters and loiterers there were at least seven men who could have been Hammers—male KGBs. They had that spook stamp. But they could also, Apple was aware, be newspaper reporters, burglars or innocent bystanders.

Each of the suspect seven, plus several other people, became more alert when now Alicia Suvov appeared beyond the row of glass doors, alighting from a taxi. She looked attractive, even imposing, in a blazer and flannel skirt.

Behind her came a muscular, flat-faced woman in a smock whom Apple immediately christened Babushka, so strongly did her form and features call out for peasant dress and a headscarf.

Followed by a suitcase-toting porter, the two women made an understated entrance. Alicia Suvov neatly side-stepped a man who moved into her path, turned her face from the flash of a camera aimed by another man, pushed between chatting women and reached the reception desk.

Both those men had been of the suspect seven, Apple noted. He put a tick beside the mental image he had retained of them, which gave him a feeling of having made progress. This helped to counter his dejection at how efficiently and effectively the lady had dealt with would-be interceptors.

There seemed to be more of the same coming now, as four young bespectacled people, three boys and a girl in their late teens, moved up into a line behind Alicia Suvov. Business at the desk finished, she turned to leave. Unexpectedly, she paused. She listened to the quartet, smiled and began to converse, with Babushka standing patiently by.

The four were students of Russian, Apple concluded. Too bad the language angle had been vetoed by God Watkin, except as a final move.

Apple swivelled on his stool, sipped the drink, wondered why, when he left university, he hadn't gone into foreign banking in Tahiti, or teaching languages somewhere like the French Riviera; sipped the drink so many times that he felt the picture must look peculiar, all liquid gone; shook his glass while staring at it closely as if he had just discovered that people breathe.

After spending an immense amount of time with the youngsters, Apple thought, not noting that it was almost as much time as he needed to spend with her himself, Alicia Suvov moved off towards the stairs, her entourage still including the laden porter.

The young quartet turned towards Apple, leaving. Each youngster wore a round lapel badge, Apple saw. He got up to go over for a closer look. A voice from behind seared him with a callous "Just a minute." He looked back. The waitress said, "You didn't pay for your drink."

With a grade-five tingling on his neck, Apple thrust her money enough for two orange juices and told her to keep the change. Himself he told sarcastically that he was doing a great job of low-profiling.

And now he had to hurry, which he did while trying to look casual. Body still and feet on a scurry, he reached the entrance wall just as the four youngsters were nearing. He saw that their badges bore only initials: ASFC.

It took Apple five seconds to work that one out. Sagging at the knees, he stopped the last of the youths to pass by with "Excuse me, sir." Always give the young age, and the old youth.

Perkily, eagerly: "Yes?"

"You're in the Alicia Suvov Fan Club, of course. I've had your literature and I'm thinking of joining."

"Good for you."

"But first, while she's in London, I'd like to get every glimpse I can of Miss Suvov."

"Naturally," the fan said. "And there's the tournament."

"I'll be leaving town before then," Apple said. "So I was wondering if you could give me an idea of Miss Suvov's movements over the next couple of days."

Obviously pleased at being able to show off his inside information, the fan said, "She only has one firm engagement. That's dinner with the executive committee of the Alicia Suvov Fan Club, tonight. Otherwise she'll just be coming and going, I suppose."

Lose one, win one, Apple was thinking a minute later as he strode along the street. He hadn't learned a thing that was helpful but at least he had found his grabber. Lemon marmalade strikes again.

It took longer than expected, an hour, to locate the right kind of shop, the right size of badge, the white paint used by typists who didn't like x-ing out, the initials to stick on. With the finished product in his pocket, feeling clever, Apple returned to Viscount Tower, where he learned from a snatch of overheard slander that Icy Alice had just left.

During the long afternoon Apple came and went, waiting inside and outside and along the street. He wasn't bored. This was, after all, a bona fide espionage mission, or anyway connected with one. In addition, he covertly practised pin-sticking the badge swiftly in place on his left-breast pocket, as well as sometimes waiting along the street at tease-danger range. Once he even went into a fast-fooder and ate a hamburger, choking.

The scene at Viscount Tower remained the same, with one or more of the suspect seven present, whom Apple now thought of as the Seven Dwarfs. They were all there at dusk when Alicia Suvov and her companion returned, by taxi.

Two of the men beat Apple in moving outside. He was still getting his badge out as, with a neat little twirl, the chess star swung around the pair and left them with Babushka. She, face friendly, pushed straight between and followed Alicia inside.

Apple was about to do the same when a man moved in front of him and said, "Hold it."

One of the Seven Dwarfs, he was six feet tall, thirty or so and plain of face. He had foxy, restless eyes like a repeat cuckold.

Apple put his badge-holding hand back in his pocket, which move made Foxy twitch. He said, "Watch it."

"Hold it and watch it," Apple said pleasantly. "This all sounds a bit peculiar."

"Never mind the brilliant humour. Just tell me what you're up to with your loitering."

"What's it got to do with you?"

"I'm Security here," Foxy said. "That's what. And if I were you, I'd piss off before I call the cops."

Apple stopped feeling facetious. This could be awkward. Not that he necessarily accepted the man as legitimate, but he might be, and the last thing you did on a caper was get involved with the law.

"Maybe I'll go to the cops myself," he said mildly, drawing away. He began to whistle.

The man followed. "What d'you mean?"

"Nothing, nothing." He went on across the forecourt.

Foxy, behind, began to speak, but what he said was swamped by the roar of a motor-cycle. That, almost at once, was topped by a screech of brakes. That, immediately, was joined by a raucous yell.

Apple stopped and twisted around.

Roar, screech and yell gone, there was silence for the tableau: Foxy on the ground, face twisted with pain, hands tenderly holding his knee; the motor-cyclist, helmeted like an astronaut, looking over the front of his machine at the man he had struck.

The silence broke. Cyclist and Foxy began shouting at each other about not looking where they were going, and people asked air what had happened as they came rumpling forwards with expressions of concern to conceal the excitement.

Apple, thoughtful, backed off. He turned away on the pavement and set off for Ethel through the gloaming. He had had enough for one day.

It wasn't until he had almost reached the spot where Ethel stood that Apple sensed he had a tail. There was no doubting that familiar sensation of a finger stroking the shoulders, and a fast glance behind showed a crawling car. As well as its driver, there was a passenger in the back.

Apple kept on going past Ethel.

Ahead were traffic lights, where a green man in a walking pose blinked on and off. When Apple arrived at the junction, the man turned an angry crimson. Obeying because it suited him, Apple stopped and looked back casually.

The tail car was coming, still at a crawl. Though visibility was poor due to dusk and the drab street-lighting, Apple did manage to make out that the black car's rear seat no longer had a passenger.

They had split up to double the shadowing chances, he thought. And rightly. It was a pro operation.

Leaving the traffic lights, Apple stayed on the same pavement and went around the corner. He strode out smartly. At the next corner he took another left, went midway along the block, entered an alley.

The first garbage can he came to in the dimness, he shifted with a huge swing into the service lane's centre. He did the same with two more cans before coming near to where the alley ended. There, he looked back.

A man was approaching at the far end, while behind him a car oozed by on the roadway. Seen only in silhouette (which dramatic effect Apple enjoyed), the man was tall and wore a cap.

That took care of the car, Apple thought as he moved jauntily on. He came out onto a street and crossed diagonally to another alley. This one he ran along. He heard sounds of chase.

Not until he had put several streets and service lanes between himself and where the car had been on last sighting did he slow.

During that run, Apple had started to consider ways of finding out something about the people behind, but had decided against the project. He didn't want to risk an involvement that could work against him. There was also the spook adage: Never assume that the other man knows you're only being nosy.

Apple bore another adage in mind now. It said that a right-handed person should never look over his left shoulder if walking; the movement would look awkward, which awkwardness could be imputed to some other source, possibly aggressive in nature. Also, the person could lose his balance.

Apple looked over his right shoulder. He saw no signs of the man in the cap. Stopping, he went through the ritual of lighting a cigarette.

Apple got pleasure out of every second of the act, in particular the way he cupped his hands to keep the flame's light from shining on his face. It came almost as an interference, the information supplied by the routine, that the man was still back there.

Apple walked on.

He had no worry about his cigarette-lighting being given the wrong interpretation. In the espionage world, that act was no longer used as a body-language signal, having been rendered obsolete by mass employment.

Around the next corner, on a busier road lined with shops, Apple saw a taxicab rank on the other side and further along. He smiled. The set-up was perfect for Routine Eight.

Moving along beside the closed business places, he didn't bother to check on whether or not he still had his shadow: the man would be there.

Four taxies were standing in the line-up. The first drove off now with a customer and the rest moved along one place. The leader was stopping as Apple drew level with it. He set off across the road.

The beauty of Routine Eight, he mused, was that if it didn't come off you hadn't lost anything—apart from a little esteem in the eyes of your tail.

Apple came to the cab's roadway side. He got in the rear. As he closed the door he said, "Viscount Tower. I'm not going but I want you to pick up a lady there. She ought to be waiting outside."

"Well now," the driver said in a grey tone.

Apple handed over two pound notes. "If she's not there, and you'll know her by her green punk hair-do, forget the whole thing and keep the money. Okay?"

Pinkly: "That's fine by me."

"Right," Apple said. He opened the other door and crouched out of the taxi. "Good night."

Staying low, buttocks and heels on close terms, Apple shut the door and stumped his awkward way to the inside of the pavement. Briefly, he was annoyed at himself for feeling relieved because there were no observers at hand.

The shoe store had a recessed entrance. After penetrating its semi-darkness, Apple peered out at the street. The taxicab he had sent after a tame goose was just driving out of sight. In the other direction, the man with a cap was arriving from across the street at cab number two. Before it could shunt up to the lead spot, he opened the door and got in. The taxicab moved on at once.

As soon as it had gone from his restricted view, Apple came out of his hiding place. Rising to three-quarters of normal height, he began walking. He walked in the same direction as taken by the two taxicabs.

It wouldn't take long, Apple knew, for the shadow to cotton on to the fact that there was no passenger in the taxi he was following. Initially he would have failed to concern himself with this because he had accepted that his mark was in the cab. Such acceptance is the basis of all theatrical illusions.

Apple had covered only half a block when he saw the tailing cab's stop lights flick on. He went into another doorway, where he stood small and with his face averted.

A moment later, the man in the cap came along at a run. Still mostly a silhouette, he went straight on by. He was following his natural assumption that his mark, having given him the slip, had gone in the opposite direction.

When Apple came out, his shadow had gone. He walked on at a brisk pace. He hummed. He was happy.

TWO

An idea for the cornering of Alicia Suvov, so that he could use his grabber of being a member of her fan club, came to Apple as soon as he entered Viscount Tower the next morning. At that moment, seeing the lobby again, he remembered the Russian women having used the stairs yesterday, not the lifts.

Which memory, he mused, he owed to the fact that, being so tall, he had been able to see over intervening people.

Wondering how he could apprise Angus Watkin of that goody, Apple began to circle the lobby at an innocuous dawdle, meanwhile bending at the knees and wearing a faint, old-nun smile.

In picking out the Six Dwarfs as he went (Foxy was missing), Apple reminded himself that, since the public chat with Alicia Suvov was patently for an observer's benefit, some or all of these loiterers could be here for precisely that reason. He shouldn't read danger into everything. Furthermore, motor-cycle accidents could happen to anyone and people often got tailed by mistake.

His smile grown sour, Apple reached the stairs and went up. He stopped as soon as he was around the first corner, with another corner ahead. Here, unseen from above or below, he would wait for the chess star.

The idea had drawbacks, Apple allowed, one being that he might well wait for ever. But it was a better plan than any of those which had resulted from his overnight think-

ing, after he had accepted that he couldn't simply go on
hanging around the lobby. The most feasible idea had
been falling into a faint in the lady's path, which, if nothing else, had afforded Apple a good deal of amusement at
its silliness.

Time passed.

Apple stood, sat, paced out the three-stride trip back
and forth across a carpeted step. Occasionally he massaged
the elbow he had bruised last night while he had been
practising faints.

People came by, going up or down. Whenever that happened, Apple pretended to be tying his shoelace. What he
would do if he got repeat custom, he didn't know. It gave
him something to fret about.

Voices sounded above. Apple tensed for action again,
either to get out his Alicia Suvov Fan Club badge or to
stoop over a shoe. The voices, nearer, belonged to two
females. Apple unbent his knee and reached for his hip
pocket.

Right around the corner now, the voices were speaking
in Russian.

Apple turned away while pulling out the badge. He had
it pinned firmly into place by the time he had gone down
the steps and around the corner.

In view of the lobby, Apple again turned. He set himself
for an upwards-seeming movement, his arms frozen on
the swing.

The women were about to appear above, their voices
clear. One was saying, ". . . any of those fan-club idiots,
dear. Such a nuisance."

Apple's response was as immediate as if to a kick. He
slapped a hiding hand fast and hard to the badge on his
breast pocket. There he held himself as the two women
came into view around the corner.

Alicia Suvov and Babushka took two steps down before

coming to a stop, just above where Apple stood in his pose. They looked at him and they looked at each other and they looked at him once again.

As a muttered and amused aside, Alicia Suvov said, still in Russian, "Did you ever see such a picture of total sincerity?" Babushka giggled.

Apple didn't know what his face showed, but he did realise that he was standing there in a forward lean with a hand over his heart.

Easing upright, he asked, "I beg your pardon?"

Alicia Suvov shook her head. "It was nothing." She spoke in English. "Is something wrong?"

"As a matter of fact," Apple said, neatly dropping his thumb on the inside of his flat hand and gripping the badge, "you startled me."

"Why is that?"

"I don't know what to say." This was true.

Alicia Suvov still looked lightly amused. She also looked more attractive than in her photograph. The features were softer, the eyes a langorous grey.

Head aslant, she asked, "I startled you and you do not know what to say?"

Having eased the badge out of its place, Apple brought his hand down. He put the failed brilliant idea away as he said, "You have grey eyes just like my mother."

In her own language Babushka said nonchalantly, "That one's been used before, dear. He's obviously a reporter."

In Alicia Suvov's face, the amusement slipped away like folk before a collection-box. More in resignation than annoyance she said, "The *Times?* Washington *Post? Newsweek?*"

Apple shook his head three times. "No. No. No."

"You want to splash me on the front page? You wish me to comment on the new Geneva crisis?"

Now Apple saw a way. Though far from perfect, it was the only way he had. He said with a touch of pride, "I, Miss, am with the West Danglington *Weekly Crier*."

"The what?"

"And you, of course, must be the very person I was just looking for. If, that is, you were talking Russian a moment ago."

"We were."

Apple smiled broadly. "Then this is your lucky day."

Alicia Suvov asked a cold "My lucky day?"

"Yes. I'll tell you how it is. My editor asked me to do an interview with Maria Kowski, the tennis player—and I suppose you'll have heard the story on *her*."

Both women shook their heads and said an interested "No."

"It's quite a scandal."

Babushka: "What is it?"

"Well," Apple said. "But please let me explain first. It was after I found out that Miss Kowski isn't available, sad to say, that I was told of this Russian chess player, and I thought she'd do nicely. I don't know a thing about chess, but I don't see how that'll make much difference, do you?"

Again both women shook their heads, the movement as devoid of animation as their expressions.

"So I'll tell you what, Miss Suvemov."

"Suvov," Babushka said.

"That's right," Apple ran on. "So what I'll do is, I'll do an interview with you, and when it's published I'll send you several copies." He smiled up benevolently.

The chess star began to show moderate amusement again. She said, "I am sorry to tell you that I do not grant interviews. However, I thank you for your kind offer."

"The West Danglington *Weekly Crier* is a very good newspaper, I'd like to mention."

"I am sure it is."

"We have a circulation of twelve thousand four hundred," Apple said. "Almost."

"That is admirable, Mr.—"

Apple started to pronounce his real last name, then caught himself half-way through, resulting in a drawn-out "Po-o-or . . ." He sounded like a Southerner calling for his father.

"Poor," Apple amended. "As in downtrodden. Jeff Poor."

"How do you do, Mr. Poor."

"Hello, Miss Suvov. I'm quite a good newspaperman."

Alicia said graciously, "I am sure you are, Mr. Poor. It is too bad we cannot help each other."

"But look. Maybe I can buy you a coffee and simply chat to you. I could make an article out of that. And I'll tell you what I'll do."

"What will you do, Mr. Poor?"

"I'll send you ten copies. *Ten.*"

"That is more than generous. However . . ."

Acting as though everything were settled, grinning like a new father, Apple went up to stand on the same step as the chess star. She looked up at him with a flick of surprise. "You *are* tall, Mr. Poor."

Apple said yes, Babushka said they had to be going, Alicia said she was right.

"And just think," Apple said, "if I'd used the lift instead of the stairs I would've missed you. Finally my claustrophobia did me a favour."

Alicia Suvov smiled. "I have that problem myself."

"You don't say."

"Also I am afraid of the dark."

Clever, not being overly agreeable, Apple said, "I'm afraid of dozens of things."

Babushka took a step downwards. "We were going to

have a coffee anyway, dear," she said in Russian. "Ask him about that Maria Kowski."

Which Apple wormed out of by saying rumour whispered that the tennis player had used drugs at Wimbledon last year. Babushka lost interest.

By that time they were sitting on stools in the coffee shop. They had been served, Apple had put money into the taut hand thrust out by the purse-mouthed waitress, had recovered from that and was telling himself with a growing pleasure, *Five minutes at least. Only ten to go.* He had finished telling himself that it was ridiculous to feel that he was starting vicious gossip.

Alicia, in the middle, said, "I want to hear more of your marvellous newspaper, please, Mr. Poor."

As slowly as he could without sounding as if he were falling asleep, Apple talked about the West Danglington *Weekly Crier.* In the main he drew on old movies about crusading small-town papers with dashing reporters and crotchety but golden-hearted editors. He grew quite involved.

Babushka looked at her watch. Coming back from the roar of the presses, Apple thought, *Seven minutes to go.* He said, "And the circulation continues to grow."

Between sips of coffee, Alicia Suvov murmured, "Fascinating." She had said it before at regular intervals, and this time, it seemed to Apple, the word had become more of a clang than a chime.

The best way to hold a person's interest is to be that person's audience. Remembering the adage from Training Four, Apple said, "Tell me, Miss Suvov, do others in your family have grey eyes?"

A grandmother, a sister and two nephews, Alicia reported. She gave their names, ages and birth signs, went

on to talk of the boys' skill at chess. Apple said perhaps it
had something to do with the grey eyes.

Five minutes to go, he thought. He made a fast scan of the
lobby while pretending to swivel his neck in his collar.
The Dwarfs were watching. They looked as pleased as if
someone were stealing their diamond mine.

Babushka said, "Don't forget the time, dear."

"No," Alicia Suvov said. She took a gulp of coffee.

His voice louder, Apple asked, "What's your birth sign,
Miss Suvov?"

"Pisces," she said. "And, curiously enough, my nephews
are the same, as I just mentioned."

"What about your mother and father?"

Warmly, Russianly, Alicia began to talk about her parents, Apple nodding her on with fixed gaze and ajar
mouth as though it were the most riveting story he had
ever heard.

Babushka stopped drumming fingers and performed a
pointed look at her watch. Alicia took no notice. Apple's
response was to think, *That must be enough. Fifteen minutes.*
Sagging happily, he dropped his hypnotised-rabbit expression. *Mission completed.*

"And then when they put him in charge of production,"
Alicia was saying, still with her father, "things started to
hum." She frowned prettily. "Is that the correct idiomatic
phrase?"

"It certainly is," Apple said. "Your English is excellent.
Congratulations."

"Thank you, Mr. Poor."

"It's a difficult language."

"I agree. So when are they going to simplify the spell-
ing, at least?"

Relaxed, confident as a swindler, Apple joined in an attack on the insanity of written English. From there they
shared an appreciation of Dickens.

He liked the chess star a lot, Apple decided. She was far warmer than expected, as well as less pompous, less the sought-after celebrity. He mused that if they had met under different circumstances, they might have become close. Already they were using their eyes in a slightly more intimate way than the normal.

Apple was sorry, as well as surprised, when Babushka said in Russian, "We've been here half an hour, dear." She got up. "We must write those letters."

In the same language Alicia said, fondly, "What a fusspot you are." She slid her coffee cup away and rose.

"Well, thank you for your time, Miss Suvov," Apple said as he pushed up from the stool. "It was a pleasure talking to you."

"And you, Mr. Poor."

They shook hands. "I hope you enjoy your stay in London."

"Thank you, but I have been here before, of course. I have seen all the sights. There is nothing new left for me here, unfortunately."

On the hook of the moment Apple said, "I know something you might not have seen."

"I doubt it, Mr. Poor. I have visited palaces and museums, monuments and zoos, and whatever else one can think of. I have been everywhere."

"Have you been inside a real English country cottage?" he asked, mock-imperious.

With Babushka hovering impatiently, Alicia gave slow nods. She said, "Yes, that is something which I have not experienced. Is it where serfs dwelled?"

"Not quite. It's only a couple of hundred years old. Would you like to see it? It's not a museum. It's mine. My home on weekends."

"That sounds most charming, Mr. Poor."

Apple bowed. "Then, Miss Suvov, I hereby invite you
to tea in the country."

Alicia asked a prompt "When?"

"Anytime you want. How about today?"

Again promptly: "I accept. Thank you."

They exchanged smiles, proud parents of an accord. Apple said, "I'll pick you up at three, if that's all right."

"Perfectly," Alicia said. "But if you do not mind, it
would be better if we met away from here."

"It would?"

"Yes. Because of the press and so forth."

"I'm afraid I don't understand, Miss Suvov. Reporters?"

"Among others," the chess star said. She smiled in apology like a good winner. "They bother me quite a lot."

"I wonder why," Apple said in his rôle of the innocent
Jeff Poor. "It's not as though you're famous or anything."

Babushka turned away with coughing sounds. Alicia
Suvov said, "It is a poor season for news, I imagine. But
about our meeting this afternoon."

They agreed on a square that lay a two-minute walk
from the rear of the building. Apple said, "I hope these
people don't follow you, annoy you."

"Oh, I shall leave by the back door. We do that when we
are not in the mood for playing untouchable. Until three,
Mr. Poor."

Like a dancer exiting to fat applause at stage left, Apple
went outside in a swirl of pleasure. He had pulled off a
difficult piece of caper business with plus-success, and he
had managed to make a date with an attractive, sociable,
brilliant woman. As an aside, Apple ordered himself not
to give another thought to the maligned Maria Kowski.

He whistled his way across the forecourt. It was only as
he reached the street that he realised what his date im-
plied. The whistle squirted off.

Porter, Appleton, was continuing an association that was initially part of an espionage operation. Could be he would rip the cloak or blunt the dagger.

Therefore should he, Apple wondered, call in? Report? Let Angus Watkin know about the afternoon meeting?

Negative, Apple thought. Watkin would almost certainly order that the date be cancelled, that his underling stay well away from the subject, that he stop behaving in an unprofessional manner. So there would be no report. And since one hadn't been asked for—no sweat.

In any case, Apple assured himself knowingly, the operation couldn't be hurt by the cottage visit, surely. Alicia Suvov was merely a peripheral figure in the drama.

Feeling brave and rebellious, as well as a clever spook and a success with women, Apple was amenable when a man stopped him with "Excuse me."

"I don't think I can help you, sorry," Apple said. "I'm a stranger here myself."

"No, it's not that," the man said. He, Apple now saw, was one of the Dwarfs. As neatly dressed as a dummy in a window, he had a round, pleasant face and a lot of smile.

"I'm Ben Rogers, legman for TV-East's 'This Week' show. You've probably heard of it."

"Yes, Mr. Rogers, I probably have."

"Well, the point is, I saw you talking with Alicia Suvov in the lobby there."

"Ah," Apple said as slowly as a yawn. Could this, he questioned, be part of the main operation? Was this the observer for whom the quarter-hour chat had been set up? If so, what was the reaction supposed to be?

The man said, frowning with interest at what he was saying while not losing a gram of smile, "I was wondering if Miss Suvov was an old friend of yours."

"I see, I see. May I ask why you were wondering about that, Mr. Rogers?"

"It's connected with a profile on her, a documentary we're preparing. If you're important in the Suvov story, Mr.—um—"

Apple asked, "If I'm important, what?"

Smooth over the name snub, the man said, "Then I know we'd like to feature you in the documentary."

"You mean have me on television?"

"Exactly. For a fee, I hasten to add. If you like, we could go to the studio at once. Discuss the matter. See the producer. My car's along here."

Before Apple had even started to think of a suitable response, the man jerked as if startled, at the same time gasping, "Careful!"

The blow caught Apple on the upper biceps. It was powerful enough to knock him off balance, so that he stumbled against a kerb-parked vehicle. Recovering there, he swiftly took in the surrounding scene.

Standing back with a surprised, unsmiling expression was the man called Rogers. Nearer, wearing overalls, was a man with a ladder. He had it resting horizontally across his shoulder. The ladder it was that had hit Apple—and he realised that if he had been of normal height, he would have received a nasty crack on the head. As it was, the pain in his shoulder was strong.

In his twenties, beery-faced, the man with the ladder was apologising anxiously between asking a repeated "Are you all right, mate?"

"Perfectly," Apple lied every time.

Huffing, Rogers said, "You ought to be more careful."

"I try. But this always happens when you carry ladders. You turn around, forgetful-like, and somebody gets bashed."

Apple rubbed his arm. "I know how it is. Don't worry."

"Well, if you're sure you're okay," the man with the ladder said, hefting his burden, "I'll get on me way." He took two steps, started to turn with a final word—and the swinging ladder cracked against the television man's head.

The thunk coincided with Apple's shout of warning. The next sound, following immediately, was that of the injured man falling to the ground like a bag of lead soldiers.

When Apple got to him and bent over, he was unconscious, sprawled on his back, face pale. Apple loosened his tie while passers-by gathered above. They began to tell each other how terrible he looked, poor soul.

The victim groaned, rolling his head from side to side. Apple, who knew about these things from Training Six, said, "Wake up. Tell me your name. Come on, wake up."

A woman above said that if it was a fit, you had to put a pencil or something between the teeth. The victim groaned on, as he had every right to, Apple could see: that lump showing above his ear was no joke.

"Come on," Apple persisted. "What's your name?"

After a flicker of eyelids reminiscent of a sleeping vamp, the man stopped groaning and started in on mumbles. Apple bent closer: "What's that?"

The victim whispered, *"Je m'appelle Jean-Paul Gilot."*

Apple gave another yawn-slow "Ah." Not only was Ben Rogers a phony name, he had been using a borrowed language.

Getting up, Apple looked among the surrounding group. The man with the ladder was absent. Nor was he to be seen anywhere else along the street.

But he could still be genuine, Apple argued. And Jean-Paul Gilot could have changed name and language and citizenship for his career in television. And yesterday's motor-cycle mishap could have been accidental. Sure. And Angus Watkin could be Little Red Riding Hood.

"He's all right, be round in a minute," Apple told the fit

woman. "Hold his hand." He passed through the people and strode off, alert.

But why had the attacker tried to get him first? Apple mused. And could it have been that way with the motor-cyclist? Could both deals, in lovely fact, have been a case of the maim-not-kill striker getting the wrong man, his own man?

Or Apple wondered if this wasn't all the product of his wishful imagination. Rubbing his arm, whose damage he would add to the bruised elbow on his list of mission scars, he changed direction. He was going to detour to the park-ing spot. He didn't want to risk forming for anyone a connexion between himself and Ethel.

But a moment later Apple realised that it didn't matter. The caper was over.

At home, as he lunched on frozen pizza, Apple's thoughts about Alicia Suvov were grateful as well as scin-tillating. Without the date for tea to look forwards to, he knew he would be feeling the post-caper blues, more so as the job had been a pathetic thing in the first place.

Even so, after finishing his dessert of that last slice of lemon-marmaladed toast, Apple went to his typewriter. Under the heading *Mission Expenses*, he put down the or-ange juice (true price, not what he had given) and the two pounds he had paid to the tame-goose cabbie. It wasn't much, but better than nothing at all.

While crossing the room, intending to look at the paper in his typewriter from a different angle, Apple's eye fell on the telephone. He went there and got to work.

It took nine calls to establish that yes, a Ben Rogers worked for TV-East, and that no, Mr. Rogers was not available, because of the fact that he was still in Australia.

But the caper was over. Apple tore up his expense sheet and went to fix coffee.

"Ethel. It is such a beautiful name."

"Thank you."

"Almost as beautiful as she is herself. I have never seen anything quite like her, and I have been everywhere in the world."

His head lolling slightly, Apple said, "Oh well."

"There is nothing like her in Russia, I can assure you."

Passenger on the pull-down seat, Apple at the wheel, they were bowling along on a thruway at sixty miles an hour. Ethel trembled as though doing a hundred. But Apple had less concern for his vehicle than he had for Alicia, who was clinging to the window-frame behind him.

At the risk of being a bore on the subject, he asked again, "Sure you're all right?"

"Perfectly. It is kind of you to worry."

"You'd be far better off on the real seat."

"But, Mr. Poor, this reminds me of those fairground rides when I was a girl. I like it."

"Fine," Apple said. He took Ethel around a bend. "You know, people in this country are pretty informal nowadays. Why don't you call me by my first name."

"Thank you," the chess star said. "I shall. And you must call me by mine."

Progress, Apple thought. But it had all gone smoothly, right from the prompt appearance of Alicia, who looked shapely-elegant in pants and sweater of clinging black wool, to the niceness of her being unaccompanied by Babushka.

Alicia said, "It would not surprise me if we had music aboard."

Apple switched on the radio. "Do you like jazz?"

"I like anything with vitality."

Nothing more was said after that, Apple having dialled his favourite station, except for when he mentioned between numbers that the rumour of drug-taking hadn't been about Maria Kowski, but someone else altogether.

With a flourish, his eyebrows raised, Apple brought Ethel to a sweeping stop on the gravel patch. They got out. Alicia's admiration of the exterior over with, they went inside to tour. Apple was as proud to act as guide as a Prado pickpocket. He also enjoyed being able to talk with little restraint, honestly. He hoped that the Jeff Poor persona wasn't going to be a nuisance.

Tour over, Apple said, "Before we have tea, I think we ought to get my dog from the farm."

Lifting her hands as if she wanted to clap, Alicia asked a delighted "You have a dog?"

On their way over the fields, Apple not only explained boarding arrangements but also told of Monico's various neuroses and oddities, from his dislike of barking to his romantic attachment to the farm cat.

At the earshot point, Apple whistled. Monico eeled through a fence and came at his loping, sideways run. The meeting was like a reunion after twenty years away, in Siberia, or so Alicia said as she stood laughingly watching.

Her having been told about Monico's personality made things easier when, while they were going back, Monico declined to chase after the stick she threw for him. Apple was tempted to play fetch himself, to make his guest happy, which brought home to him the fact that he was already midway to being smitten. He wasn't at all surprised.

With the meal of high tea, taken at the living room table, Apple served the fancy sandwiches he had laboriously made at home and the cream cakes he had bought on his way to the meeting place. Alicia said all the right things and kept Monico hovering with tid-bits.

The conversation wandered like a cheerful hobo. Once it rested on politics, but not for long, as Apple, recalling the ex-girl-friend, dragged it to its feet and pushed it on its way.

Putting down her paper napkin, Alicia said, "Wonderful. I am quite replete."

"Can't you manage another cake?"

"Thank you, Jeff, no. But a cigarette, yes."

"Didn't know you smoked," Apple said, "or I would've offered you one before."

Alicia shook her head. "I just like to hold a burning cigarette sometimes. It makes me feel worldly. Perhaps you could light one for me, please."

After lighting two cigarettes at the same time without getting smoke in his eyes, Apple handed one across with "But you are a worldly person, Alicia."

"Then possibly it is a need for pretence. Some of us need it, with others it is a social or career necessity."

"Mmmm," Apple mumbled, still thinking of how well he had done that two-cigarette bit.

Alicia said, "For example, there is yourself. All this could be pretence." She waved her cigarette like a baton at the string section.

Apple came alert. "Um—pretence?"

"Precisely, Jeff. An act."

"Some sort of social facade, I suppose you mean."

As though to give more emphasis to the negative, Alicia closed her eyes while shaking her head. "In the sense which I have in mind, no."

"I don't follow you, Alicia," Apple said, uneasy.

"What you seem to be and what you are, Jeff, could be quite different things. You seem to be a reporter, but that could be an act. Couldn't it?"

Apple covered half his face with the cigarette-holding hand in case his expression was quirky. After inhaling smoke, he blew it out with a careless "An act of what?"

"Not that I really think so," Alicia said. "Though I will admit, it did cross my mind at first, at Viscount Tower."

Persisting: "An act of what, Alicia?"

"Possibly that is why I was malleable when we met. Perhaps I wanted to see how long it would take me to trip you up, or for you to trip up yourself."

"How'm I doing?" Apple asked, with difficulty producing a smile. "At whatever it is we're talking about."

"Very well indeed," Alicia said. "I long ago decided that you can't be."

"Can't be *what?*"

She said, "With the Komitet Gosudarzstvennoi Bezopasnosti."

"Eh?"

"Or, less awkward, the KGB."

After a moment of unacted gaping, ordered by total surprise, Apple splurged into the laughter of relief. "The Russian secret police?" he asked. "The spies?"

As all along, Alicia wore a faint smile. "Yes, Jeff. The cold, grey bogeymen."

Following another pause, more floundering in the absurdity of it all, Apple asked an amused "But why would an agent of the KGB, one of your own countrymen, be talking to you in a disguise, Alicia?"

"Many reasons. To get on an intimate footing, if not to become eventually a permanent fixture. To test me for loyalty to the Soviet Union, stupid though that may seem."

"Yes, it does."

"Or," Alicia went on, "to gain my confidence and then reveal the truth and try to enlist my aid, or services, or at least sympathy. I have no patience with these people."

"I can understand that."

"Or, of course, they might try entrapment. Somehow

. try to create false evidence which they would use as a lever, force me to do their bidding."

Apple nodded. "You'd be very useful. A person in your position could pick up all kinds of information."

"Yes, I have access almost everywhere."

"I can see now why you're so wary."

Alicia conducted the strings again. "Oh, I have been through this before, Jeff."

"But are the KGB that bad?"

"All secret services are as bad as that. British, American, Chinese or what have you. The KGB, in fact, might even be the mildest of the lot."

Apple tossed his cigarette into the fireplace. "Before we go any further," he said, "allow me to show you my credentials." He reached for the inside pocket of his windcheater, which held only a chewed bus ticket. He tingled at the danger.

Making fast jabs at the trombones, Alicia protested, "No. Please. I am embarrassed."

"But to put your mind at rest . . ."

"It is at rest. Stop."

Apple let his arm fall. "If you insist."

"In any case," Alicia said, "documents are the simplest things of all to fake."

"Oh. Yes, I suppose they are."

"What is not so easy is the background. The visibles. The factors such as this cottage."

"I've been here for years," Apple said.

"But that, come to think of it, would not count you out. Moscow, they say, is full of foreign agents who have been there half their lives."

"I imagine that's true."

"But enough," Alicia said. She ended the concerto with a swipe and threw her cigarette after Apple's. "Enough talk of that dark world."

Apple said, "Sitting here, it's hard to believe it really exists." He told himself not to worry. If Alicia truly suspected him of not being what he represented, she wouldn't have mentioned it, nor would she have been so outspokenly anti-KGB.

"I believe I shall have another cup of tea," Alicia said comfortably.

She went on to talk of her family, arriving at Irini (Apple preferred Babushka as a name), a cousin, who tried to be protective, especially in respect of reporters and fans.

"Myself, I like the fan clubs," Alicia said. "In fact, I am dining with one of them this evening." She looked at her watch. "We must leave presently, Jeff."

"Whenever you like."

"But first you must show me the family album."

Apple repeated, "The family album?" He had a presentiment of something dismal.

"Yes. Photographs of your family. Your people."

"Ah yes. But I don't keep any pictures here."

"You don't?"

"No," Apple said. "Those few that I do have, they're in my London flat."

Her face becoming as expressionless as an Oriental poker player's, Alicia gazed around the walls and across the mantel. She said, "I see."

Apple laughed grindingly, like a clown at a rival's joke. "Would you say that was suspicious?"

"Not at all. In these matters, anything can be suspect."

"That's true, true, very true."

"I mean, for example, how does a reporter afford a town apartment *and* a country cottage?"

"The cottage I inherited," Apple said. This truth he spoke so sincerely that it sounded to him like a lie. "Honest."

"I believe you."

"The London place costs me the earth."

"Talking of apartments," Alicia said blandly, "how did you know the number of mine at Viscount Tower?—just for the sake of interest."

"The number?"

"You said you were on your way up to see me."

"I can explain that," Apple lied drably.

"Please do. I'd like to know the system."

Playing for time, praying for light: "How d'you mean?"

"Forewarned is forearmed, as the adage goes."

Blinking at the light, Apple said, "I simply walked up to the desk and asked. As it happens, the clerk was busy and he probably answered without thinking. I hope you're not going to get the poor man into trouble."

"No, of course not," Alicia said. She smiled. "But I must not tease you anymore. I will not even mention that I found it curious, earlier, when you changed the subject away from politics."

Apple, feeling easier, but prepared to feel terrible if she asked what the number of her apartment was, said, "I always try to do that here. Politics goes with beer, not tea."

Alicia laughed as she got up. But she had become a shade quieter than the person who had arrived, Apple thought; more like her public image. Which, he told himself, could be because she was easing back in that direction now the date was ending.

However: Alicia didn't show any interest in Monico when they took him over the fields, and when they set off in Ethel she sat on the full seat and asked for music. With regret, Apple realised there probably wasn't much future in their relationship. Alicia was too cautious, not without reason. It would take longer than a few days, or weeks, to put that caution to rest.

However again: when they reached the parklet-centred square to the rear of Viscount Tower and got out, Alicia was effusive in her thanks for the outing and even reached up a kiss for Apple's cheek. She said:

"One day we may meet again, Jeff. It is a pity I am always so busy on these short trips abroad."

It was merely a formality, Apple knew, and he knew that the chess star knew it as well when he said he would give her a call anyway. "We might be able to get together."

"One never knows, Jeff."

Driving past the suave old building that held his flat, heading for the nearby parking garage, Apple saw a familiar face. It was on a tallish, nondescript man who stood in an easy pose by the entrance of 12 Harlequin Mansions.

Although Apple could put neither name nor place to the man, even after a triple-take, he appreciated the interruption in his thoughts. He had been feeling morose over Alicia Suvov.

Declining to consider that the man could be a neighbour, Apple drove on. In the next block he turned into the mouth of his underground garage, descending. Off the ramp he went far back to the wall-spot that was marked *Porter*, the while unawarely turtling his head because of the low ceiling. He parked, switched off, got out.

With the door still open, Apple tensed. Somewhere close at hand in the silence of the gaunt garage had sounded the scrape of leather on concrete. It was as furtive as a hiss.

Eyes flicking quickly over all the nearby cars, Apple turned slowly. He had his car-keys on the ready. Any weapon was better than none and a bunch of keys in the face was a lot better than most, if it was handled right. All this was despite Apple feeling sure he was about to see the garage attendant.

He finished his turn, the leather-scrape was repeated

into a rhythm and a man walked into view from around
the next car. Across his left cheek lay a vicious scar.

He said, "Hello, old son."

Apple's tension left as rapidly as it had arrived. This
face, doubly familiar, was immediately identifiable as belonging to a colleague in the service. Apple knew him as
Bill Burton, which may even have been his real name.

Burton asked, "Did the thin cold chill run through thy
veins?"

"Too right."

"One tries to keep in practice."

They shook hands and exchanged commonplaces like
travelling salesmen. Bill Burton, a plump man of forty
whose facial scar had an innocent origin, was one of the
few operatives whom Apple knew by more than just sight.

"You're not here by accident, are you, Bill?"

"No way, old son."

Apple's smile was an act. He was realising that, of
course, his date with Alicia had been heard of by Upstairs.
He was a fool to think it could stay secret from Angus
Watkin. So the underling was in scalding water for having
interfered with an operation. He was due for a rocket, or
possibly dismissal.

Maybe the last, Apple mused, for obviously Angus
Watkin wanted to make sure of his underling's soonest
apprehension, with an agent at the house and another in
the garage—and perhaps Albert waiting outside the
United Kingdom Philological Institute.

Failing to be uplifted by the image of the tedious Albert
standing on a kerb, chilled to the marrow, Apple said, "I
suppose God wants to see me."

"That's it, old son. As fast as now. So we won't be able
to stop on the way for a pint."

"Okay. Hop in."

"No, there's a staff machine outside," Bill Burton said. "Lock up dear old Ethel and let's go."

Not at all liking the notion of being taken, rather than being asked to attend, Apple went out to the street with Bill Burton. They got in a plain black car and Burton drove along to Harlequin Mansions.

The other agent got in the back. His greeting was a grunt. When he did speak, as they were easing into the evening-rush traffic, it was to say, bitterly, "Everyone else in the bloody world has a car, and me, I have to share."

Apple had his own problems. He was unassured by Bill Burton's cheery manner, aware that the operative would know little about the situation, and might even think that his tall colleague was about to be offered a plum job. Because of that scar, an unhideable feature, he was rarely on the running team in a caper. He played courier, observer and that fearsome-looking heavy who stands silently grim in the background of set-up scenes.

The future looked sleazy, Apple thought. He really needed this debacle on top of the flop with Alicia. Everything was wrong and mundane. Here they were crawling in traffic when they should have been speeding along on rain-slicked streets.

It was no help to Apple's emotions when, the other two talking a variety of shop, maligning the car depot, he was unable to take part. Not only did he not understand the problem, he didn't even know where the depot was. And when the pair of professional espionage operatives switched to talking about football, which he didn't care for anyway, he sank into his depression like a cigarette into stew.

At length the car stopped opposite the safe house that Apple had been taken to by Albert. Bill Burton said, "Off you go, old son. Door's open. And the best of spook luck."

"Thanks, Bill," Apple said, getting out. "See you. And you."

The other agent grunted. As the car moved on, he got back to the conversation with an aghast "Call him a goal-keeper?"

Apple went to the house and pushed inside. While he was closing the door, his eyes rested by positioning on what lay in front of them, which happened to be the hat-stand.

Apple's gaze slowly changed from disinterested to curious; from there to doubting; from that to believing; from that to incredulous. At the same time, the hairs on the back of his neck got up as if they wanted to leave.

The hooks of the hat-stand held two topcoats and a sweater and a scarf. Its ledge held books and an ashtray and a wedding invitation. All these items were the personal property of Appleton Porter.

"Come in, please."

Had everything he owned been brought here for examination or something? Apple questioned as he moved along the passage towards the end doorway. He was trying to be logical while in an eerie daze, a dream-like state. Additionally, he had the creepiness of feeling that the person he would meet in the room was himself.

It came almost as a relief to see the expected, Angus Watkin, sitting as last time, even though some of the portable objects around him belonged in the Bloomsbury flat.

Apple pushed the door shut behind him. This gave him something to do when there was no answer to his "Good evening, sir." He nodded a gloomy greeting at one of his mother's water-colours on the wall.

"Report, please, Porter," Angus Watkin said abruptly. "And keep it simple."

"Report on my successful mission this morning at Viscount Tower, sir?" Apple said. Again getting no answer, he went on in a glitter, "Certainly. With pleasure. I'm so pleased that I was able to bring it off, and with such perfection. I kept the subject in conversation for thirty-three minutes, as you no doubt know, sir."

"No doubt I do," Watkin said. Unsurprisingly, there was nothing to be learned from his appearance or behaviour or what in his case passed for a facial expression, though his voice seemed to have a little more crispness than normal. "Report."

Apple gave up on wondering which of the Dwarfs was the observer, a Brit. Standing almost at attention, he related a close-up of the scene between himself and Alicia in Viscount Tower's lobby. He acted as though he expected to be congratulated, if not thanked profusely. That his possessions here appeared to be for looking at rather than scrutinizing had shown him the simpering light of hope.

"Then when the desired fifteen minutes had gone by," he said, "and nothing, but absolutely nothing had happened, I decided for the sake of the operation that I'd better keep the subject talking a while longer."

Angus Watkin asked, "Oh you did, did you?"

"Yes, sir. I'd already worked out what my part of the caper was all about."

"And what, pray, was that?"

"It was an Excuse-me Waltz."

A movement passed over Angus Watkin's brow. It was a frown, Apple knew, and he knew it could have happened because the underling was right, or because of the use of slang, which the spymaster hated.

An Excuse-me Waltz was when agent A gets the subject, to whom he is a stranger, into conversation so that agent B can make an approach, one that ignores the subject. Agent B says to his colleague, as though he were a stranger also, *Aren't you Joe . . . ?* or *Haven't I seen . . . ?* or *Did you just*

drop this . . . ? or anything else appropriate. The ploy begins ninety per cent of all street-operated confidence
tricks.

"I held on to her as long as possible," Apple said. "But
there's a limit to what one can do. In any case, by then I'd
concluded that I must be wrong about the caper after all."

Following an inward sigh, Angus Watkin said, "You are
wrong, Porter, you were right."

Apple, who had only been guessing, said, "But no agent
could have been that slow."

"He met with a minor accident outside the building."

"How curious."

"Therefore all your hard labour was in vain."

"Pity I hadn't known the score," Apple said. "We
could've tried again in the afternoon, couldn't we? Oh, but
you won't know about that, sir."

"Try not to be obscure, Porter."

"How's the agent, by the way?"

"None of your business. Get on with the afternoon."

Pretending he didn't realise that his Control was aware
of the date, though probably not what it had consisted of,
Apple told how, in the lobby, Alicia Suvov had begged to
be shown the cottage he had mentioned in one of his
many, many shrewd if not brilliant attention-holders; how
he had driven her there and brought her back and what
had transpired between; how, if he had known what the
caper was all about, he could have taken her to a public
place for another try at the Excuse-me Waltz.

His expression of I-did-*my*-bit Apple held on to only
briefly. It was so easy to overdo these things. In any case,
he knew that Angus Watkin wasn't fooled.

"So, Porter, you were in the young lady's company for
quite some time."

"Yes, sir. Several hours."

"And would you say that you were in a position to continue the relationship?"

"Absolutely," Apple said, squaring his shoulders because he knew he tended to cringe when lying.

"Or anyway," his superior said correctingly, "you think it might be possible."

"It will, sir. It will."

Evenly: "It better."

Weakly: "Yes, sir."

Angus Watkin said, "Sit down, Porter."

With alacrity, Apple moved forwards to the other armchair and sat. The danger, he assured himself, was past. Because of that accident in quotes to the operative, his date had been the right move. Not that that made the picture any clearer in respect of the main mission.

"The main mission," Angus Watkin said in his discomforting, occult way, "depended entirely on the abilities of our injured agent. He is a specialist in a particular field. He will recover soon with no ill effects, and there are in any case other people I could employ, but the basic problem of contact remains. And time is vital."

"Yes, sir," Apple said, wondering why Upstairs wanted to get close to Alicia. "The young lady isn't in London for long."

"More importantly, Porter, there's the competition. It could well be advancing while we sit here."

"I did suspect that. There were several familiar types around Viscount Tower."

"And all trying at the same time to put each other out of the picture."

"Yes, I know," Apple said. Hoping Angus Watkin would ask what he was doing, he rubbed his sore shoulder.

Not asking, Watkin said, "Espionage is a small world. It's not unusual when everyone gets the same idea at the same time. A word dropped at a cocktail party in Warsaw,

say, can start people in a dozen countries off on the same
scent."

"Quite so, sir," Apple said, although not understanding
a word. He rubbed on.

"People from Israel, East Germany and Bulgaria are believed to be interested, as well as the CIA."

"Also the French."

"Probably, Porter."

"No, sir. Definitely."

"Well yes, the one we got with a ladder might have been
replaced."

Apple dropped his hand from his shoulder. "And not
forgetting ourselves, sir. Our interest."

"Decent of you to remind me," Angus Watkin said with
a taste of drawl. "And naturally we ought to have the
edge, this being our country."

Apple stopped himself from saying that fair was fair.
He gave a companionable nod. "Exactly, sir."

"It seems we got the idea last. Perhaps source site was in
the other direction from here, or somewhere in which we
didn't have an ear."

Playing the toady, as he sometimes did with his Control,
and always forgave himself for it, Apple asked, "Is that
possible, sir? There being places beyond the reach of Upstairs?"

"Don't, Porter, be inane," Angus Watkin said, and pur-
sued, "Perhaps there was no source site. It could be that
everyone got interested with the discovery that the lady
doesn't like the dark."

Surprise helped Apple recover from the slap-down. He
asked, "The lady being Miss Suvov?"

"Yes, Porter, that same."

"But what does—?"

Cutting him off there with a blink, Angus Watkin asked,
"To which person you presented yourself as what?"

Apple talked about Jeff Poor, reporter for the West Danglington *Weekly Crier.* He thought it wisest not to mention that the chess star vaguely suspected Jeff Poor of being an agent of the KGB.

Watkin surprised again, now with a question: "Does the lady know your London address?"

"No, sir. But she knows I have one."

Angus Watkin nodded. He said, "Later you will receive your documentation for the Poor persona. It will be a brittle cover, but possibly good enough for the duration."

Apple twisted his head slightly to one side like a wary bird. He was worried that he might be mis-hearing or not understanding properly. "Yes?" he muttered.

"Yes," his Control said. "You, Porter. You have the contact, so you have the mission."

Apple, drooping into his chair, asked a feeble "The whole mission is mine?"

"It is. From now on your number-name is One. You will try to do what the injured ex-One would undoubtedly have done."

"Which is, sir?"

"Seduction," Angus Watkin said. "The seduction of Alicia Suvov."

THREE

Back in a daze, a glaze over the eyes of his mind, Apple was only mistily aware of Albert bringing in a tray and then leaving again; of being served a cup of tea by Angus Watkin; of taking slow sips.

Although this daze wasn't as eerie as the other, it did have its measure of strangeness: he, Appleton Porter, was being ordered to do what he himself so ardently desired.

By the time his cup was empty, Apple, aided by tea's stiff-upper-lip qualities and glances at his mother's landscape water-colour, had come partway into reality out of his daze. Or anyway, far enough out to feel a stab of worry when Angus Watkin said, setting down his cup heavily:

"Before we venture any further, of course, here and now, we have to find out if your relationship with the young lady is still alive."

Apple said a quasi-affable "Naturally, sir." He suspected his superior of regretting the serving of refreshments before this point had been settled.

"The telephone is on your left," Watkin said. "Please proceed as though I were not here." He put his fingertips together and looked at the ceiling.

Clearing his throat like a man handed a bill he couldn't pay, Apple reached out to the telephone on the side table and brought it closer, whereupon he realised he didn't know the number at Viscount Tower.

Colourlessly he asked, "Is there a directory around, sir?"

In a pale tone Angus Watkin told the ceiling, "He didn't

memorise the number." Voice normal, he gave a series of numbers and said, "Try that one."

Smiling with his bottom lip as though he had known all along, Apple dialled. When a voice answered, he asked to be connected with Miss Suvov's apartment. The voice wanted to know if he had Miss Suvov's personal code-number.

"Um—not at the moment," Apple said, keeping the receiver end of the hand-set pressed close to his ear.

The voice said, "Good-bye." The line clicked dead.

Smile forcefully in place, Apple lowered the hand-set with "She's gone out, sir."

Bringing his eyes down from the ceiling as if leaving angels behind, Angus Watkin asked, "And nobody knows where she's gone to?"

"*I* know," Apple said quickly, remembering. "Not many know where she's gone—none of the competition, I bet—but I do."

"Excellent, Porter. Where?"

Adding a hint of grandness to that bottom-lip smile: "The young lady is a dinner guest tonight of the executive committee of the Alicia Suvov Fan Club."

"Excellent again. And where is this dinner taking place?"

Apple let his smile and grandness go. He said, lowering his voice as though imparting gossip, "I don't know."

Angus Watkin shook his head faintly and faintly asked, "No?"

Whispering: "No. Except that more than likely it's somewhere in Hampstead."

Murmuring: "How, Porter, do you propose to go about finding the correct location?"

Apple said quietly, "I'll have to give that a bit of thought."

Breaking the peace by tapping both hands on the chair

arms as he began to get up, Angus Watkin said, "Time is in short supply, Porter. Therefore I hope you won't be too distressed if I interfere briefly in your mission."

Apple also started to rise, held at a gesture from his chief, sat again and said with a passing return of the grandness, "Feel free, sir."

Bending over the telephone, Angus Watkin dialled a sequence of numbers. When the instrument crackled to life, he said, "The chess player Alicia Suvov. She's having dinner with her fan club this evening. I want to know where. Call me back at Buckingham Palace." He put the receiver down.

"Is that the code-name of this place, sir?"

"Yes, Porter. And while we're waiting for your information, I'll show you around. You'll need to familiarise yourself with your temporary home."

"If enough of my things have been brought here, sir, that won't be difficult," Apple said, getting up to follow his superior out to the hall.

They saw Porter property in the dismal front room, marmalade with lemon flavour in the kitchen, an old leash of Monico's hanging on the banister post, more watercolours on the staircase wall, that hysterical tartan dressing gown in the bathroom.

One bedroom was for storage, another stood empty. Angus Watkin led the way into the third, master bedroom with a suggestion of ceremony in his manner.

Although larger than average, the room seemed otherwise on account of its king-size bed and the bar in one corner. The plain walls were liberally covered with decorative plates, framed animal photographs fronted with glass and brassware. The sole Porter possession present was reading matter on the bedside table.

Angus Watkin said, "It's a friendly, accommodating, relaxing sort of room, wouldn't you agree?"

"I would, sir, yes."

Watkin pointed. "Please note the horse photograph there, and the small brass bowl there, and the green plate there, and that gap between sherry bottles on the top shelf behind the bar there. Noted?"

Apple nodded at the four diverse points. "Yes, sir. Are they bugs?"

"No. That's where the cameras are hidden."

"The cameras, sir?"

"The cameras, Porter," Angus Watkin said with the patience of a pyramid.

"*Film* cameras?" Apple asked, his discomfort growing.

"The clever kind that take moving pictures, yes."

"They're working now?"

"Certainly not, Porter. They begin to operate when the door is closed and its bolt shot."

Trying to sink further into his lingering daze, for comfort and protection, Apple, seeing, mumbled, "I don't really see . . ."

Angus Watkin went behind the semi-circular bar. Head back, he leaned on it stiff of arm, as autocratic as any pub guv'nor in a slum. Apple wished he would say, "Let's have a drink and forget all this."

But Watkin said, "Perhaps I am being somewhat inexact. The cameras, Porter, are for filming bedroom activities."

"Ah."

"Soon, one hopes, they will be filming Miss Alicia Suvov and a certain Jeff Poor in the act of sexual congress."

What stopped Apple from uttering his noncommittal "Ah" again was a sudden fear. He thought he was going to blush. Then he realised that he was hot. He put a finger inside his collar.

"Yes," Angus Watkin said, "the heat is considerably

higher in this room. Otherwise the subjects who are brought here might be inclined to want their nakedness under the covers. That would not make the cameras terribly happy."

Apple loosened his tie an inch. To be on the safe side, he let a part of his mind envision the scene recommended by His Eastern Highness Prince Khan the Sage as he let penetrate the fact that he was expected to perform an act of the greatest intimacy, while naked, for the unavoidable cameras, the result to be seen by possibly hundreds of people.

Watkin asked, "You did realise, did you not, Porter, that the seduction of Miss Suvov would need to be visually transcribed in order to be of value?"

Apple swayed a huge nod. "Of course, of course." He let his tent in the desert fold itself and creep away.

"Perhaps you're wondering if you'll be able to go through with the, as it were, public performance."

He was trying not to wonder, and he gave a side sway with "Not at all, not at all."

A cough sounded. Turning, Apple saw Albert in the open doorway. He was looking at Watkin, who asked, "They found it?" The man in the blue boiler suit chanted numbers and names that ended in "Hampstead." Watkin looked at Apple, who repeated the address drably. Albert left like a wraith.

Angus Watkin put a glass on the bar. "Anything else you need to know in respect of mechanics, you will learn in due course."

Tiredly: "Yes, sir."

After pouring out a measure of whisky, Watkin toasted air and sipped. He said, "I won't encourage you to drink, Porter, since I know you don't have a head for alcohol."

Morosely: "Yes, sir."

"Now, as for the mission itself. Its purpose is no doubt obvious to you, mm?"

Uncaring, Apple said, "No, it isn't."

"Let me put it this way," his Control said. "What larger loss of Western face could there be than, say, a member of the Royal Family defecting to the Soviet Union?"

"Very little, sir."

"Reversewise, the Soviets would be handed the face-loss of many decades if, for instance, their darling Alicia Suvov were to ask for asylum in the West."

"It would, yes, be an immense blow."

"Which," Angus Watkin said after a taste of whisky, "could probably be brought about if the lady were shown a film of herself cavorting lewdly and nudely with a man, a complete reversal of what she represents to the Russian people."

"How, sir?"

"By giving the lady the choice: Defect, or have the film distributed in the USSR. Defect, or be eternally disgraced. Defect, or cease to exist as a public figure, even disappearing from the record books."

Apple nodded. "I see."

"The choice, it would seem, is obvious. But that remains to be seen. It's the first stage we are at present concerned with. Right, Porter?"

"Yes, sir," Apple said, patting himself as people do when they want to go.

"Any questions on that stage?"

"No."

Angus Watkin said, "Should you be fortunate enough or clever enough to get Miss Suvov to accompany you back here this evening, Porter, you will have to manage as best you can."

"In what sense?"

"In the art of seduction," Watkin said. "An art which, one assumes, you are not too familiar with."

"Ah."

"However, you will shortly be receiving, from an expert in that field, an education in sexual mechanics." He gestured with his glass at the doorway. "Off you go, Porter."

Sitting slumped in a taxi bound for Hampstead, feeling insulted and abused, soiled and used, Apple reviewed the situation. In order to be more intimate, more honest with himself, he closed his eyes.

Whether or not he could bring himself to perform in a privately made erotic movie, that Apple put aside. Not only was it another matter entirely, it took second place to a far more important consideration.

He, Appleton Porter, was expected to help in the downfall of an innocent person. That she happened to be a female, one whom he knew personally and liked, was beside the point, though it did add to the affair's sliminess.

He was being asked to disgrace this person in the eyes of her countrymen, or offer her the possibly worse shame of defection, which also meant that she would never see her family or homeland again, and there were few things worse than that for a Russian, to whom the word "exile" had a particularly pernicious connotation.

And for what? Was it because of a crisis? Was it to aid the nation in a time of war? Was it to save lives?

Apple shook his head stoutly.

No, the extortion was to be used merely for playing one more round in the spy game. This time the prize was a chess player, nice change from scientists and ballet dancers and poets. A neat strategy—the espionage services of several countries wanted the prestige of having pulled it off—and never mind what happened in the long-term afterwards to the prize.

This, Apple told himself, was not the right spy attitude. But then, he thought, he wasn't the right material for a spy in the first place.

Discomfited by all this honesty, Apple sat up, opened his eyes and straightened his tie. With folded arms he faced the question of what he was going to do.

After a minute he came to the firm conclusion that he didn't know yet. So that was a start, he thought. Now he was getting somewhere. And, of course, it had already been settled without debate that he had no intentions of playing male lead to Alicia in Angus Watkin's colour production. It just wasn't going to happen.

But he did want to keep the caper alive for as long as possible, he did want to get on a closer footing with Alicia and at the same time he did want to, had to, must, keep her from falling into other, predatory hands.

As abruptly as a flick on the nose, while thinking of those predators, Apple realised that his cogitating had been unnecessary, born of vanity. It was like worrying about getting caught afterwards if you were to go out and steal the Crown Jewels, just like that.

Apple began to blush at his audacity.

Standing in its own grounds in a quiet street, it was one of those giant blocks of flats built in a style of Tudor which the Tudors would have thought Japanese. The main doors were open, the garden had floodlights and there was a uniformed policeman at the gate.

Scene assessed as the taxi went by (in true spook fashion, despite his murky emotions, he hadn't given the right house number), Apple thought about that constable. Policemen, he was assured in knowing, always regarded him with approval, before they became wary, relating his height and neatness of dress to the fact that they could easily go with the title of Inspector.

But Apple decided against using the second element, pulling imitation rank in order to smooth his way inside; he knew he would be doing so mostly out of a wish to pass on the submission which had just been handed to him by Angus Watkin, sing the pecking-order blues. And the song could finish up badly for some poor sod somewhere.

Therefore when Apple went striding back after having paid off the cabbie, he had his Alicia Suvov Fan Club badge pinned prominently in place and his face full of self-importance, as well as special knowledge, like a bank manager's wife. Watching, the policeman slowly stood taller.

Apple reduced his pace as he drew near. He asked ahead of himself a brisk "Everything okay at this point, officer?"

With his arm giving a flap like an early-aborted salute, the constable said an uncertain "Yes, sir."

"Good for you. Keep up the good work. I'll mention it to the Super when I see him later."

"Thank you, sir."

Apple, who hadn't stopped, went on by and through the gate. As he walked the five-metre pathway, eyebrows up in the middle at his smartness, he thought he glimpsed a movement among the bushes. He hoped he wasn't mistaken.

Inside, in a hall with an unoccupied porter's desk, it came to Apple that he had forgotten the flat number. Under those dingy circumstances in the bedroom, he reasoned, eyebrows normal, it was brilliant of him to have retained any detail of the address, especially since it had been spat out by Albert as though it were bits of tobacco on his tongue.

Behind the desk hung a name-board. Apple, however, didn't have a name he could match. Shrugging, he took the stairs to the first floor. Along a passage in either direction lay dim desertion. But there wasn't a complementing silence. Apple listened while taking off and putting away his badge. The rumble of talk was coming from above.

He went up to the next floor. Along one arm of the passage, its lights on, ten or fifteen people standing around a doorway formed the obvious tip of a crowdberg.

They were not talking chess, though, Apple heard after he had come to a casual hover. The subject was whether or not a certain someone had been a burglar, a reporter, a rival or one of those awful people from the Limehouse fan club. Apple had found the right flat.

The someone under discussion, he learned after more hovering, was a man who had fallen from where he had been climbing up a drainpipe outside, following a yell as if he had been hit by something; a man who had done a bunk before the sent-for constable had arrived to investigate.

With knowing nods, given for himself to appreciate, Apple smiled his way to the door, got no smiles in return, passed through and into a room awash with people. He held his elbows out above heads as he went on, wading.

Bishops and pawns as well as burglars and rivals figured in the talk here, among studious-looking people who were drinking and smoking. Apple, getting a fair measure of the smoke, reckoned them to be post-dinner guests. Ahead lay a large, interior doorway that the standers were eyeing covetously.

Giving gentle coughs, Apple waded on until brought to a stop by a hand on his arm and a sharp voice saying, "Just a moment." He looked down.

It was that bespectacled youth to whom he had spoken in the lobby of Viscount Tower, when asking about the chess star's schedule. The young man was holding one arm of his eye-glasses as though to keep them from trembling at the ferocity of his stare.

"Ah, it's you, sir," Apple said. "Glad you could make it."

"Neat move," the young man grated. "But a loser."

"I'm usually late myself for weddings, but with this being dear old Nora's . . ."

"This, as you know very well, is not a wedding, though it is a private function. Members only. You will have to leave. You see, I know you're not a member."

The noise level was high enough for Apple to pretend not to have heard. Sagging comfortably, he said, "Listen, sir, I was joking about weddings. Fact is, I thought I'd drop in and have a word with Miss Suvov."

"That's precisely what one hundred other people would like to do," the young man said, releasing his glasses as though the matter was closed and Apple had disappeared.

"Drop in?"

"Chat with Miss Suvov. You will have to go."

"Just a little word or two, sir."

"Do you think you have more right than the others?"

Uncomfortably, Apple saw the justice in that. With a loose smile he said, "No, but it's important. I mean it's important for Miss Suvov. In regards to her safety." He had no idea where he was leading himself.

The young man put both hands to his spectacles as if using binoculars. "Safety?" There was a new squeak in his voice, a new gleam in his eyes.

"Who do you think that character was who did the climbing bit outside?"

"In my own opinion, a press photographer."

"Wrong," Apple said. "I can see I shall have to take you into my confidence, sir."

"Do, yes do."

"It was me. I'm in charge of security, y'see. I was merely checking you out when I talked to you in the Viscount lobby."

"You mean . . . ?"

"Yes," Apple said, not really knowing what he meant. But he had to avoid a scene by keeping the youth mentally off-balance. He couldn't stand scenes. "And now I must see Miss Suvov. It's urgent. So excuse me, please."

"I'll take you," the young man said. "Follow me." He turned away with a crisis mouth. Before he surged expertly into the crowd, he offered back, "Even though you have an odd way of addressing people, I didn't figure you for a Russian secret-service man."

"No no no," Apple got out; but it was too late. The youth had forged ahead and out of earshot, aiming for the interior doorway. Lumpily Apple began to follow. He had the awful sensation that he had just Biblical-sensed the whole thing.

Reaching the doorway, the young man went from sight. It took some time for Apple to get there. When he did, and passed through, it was to come face to face with Alicia.

"I knew it," she said. "When he told me that there was a KGB man here to see me . . ."

"I can explain," Apple said.

". . . I knew it had to be you," Alicia finished. She laughed with merry eyes, which act commanded grins on all those around her, including the young man. "You are naughty to tease me, Jeff."

"Tease you," Apple mumbled through the smile he was trying to flicker on. "Quite."

"I realised after we parted today, of course, how silly I had been about the KGB. I wanted to apologise. However, I did not know how to contact you."

Firming himself: "No, that's right."

"You are not in the telephone book."

"Ex-directory," Apple said at a snap. The people at hand were soft-clamouring for Alicia's attention.

She said, "Therefore I hereby apologise, even though I

must point out that it was also naughty of you to come here in the first place."

Apple ignored a faint twinge of guilt about taking up the fans' time with their idol by reminding himself of how shrewd he had been with that KGB angle.

He said, "You're right, Alicia. I return your apologies a thousand times. If you tell me when I can see you again, I'll leave like a flash."

Alicia hesitated. She made a hefting, helpless gesture with both arms as though wondering which cream pie to throw first, the while nodding vaguely at her ring of clamourers.

Apple said, "I might as well admit to having discovered that you're quite famous."

"Only a little."

"I hope you don't think my interest in you is because of that."

"Oh no," Alicia said, looking shocked.

"I'd just like to get to know you better. This isn't newspaper work."

"Of course not."

"So just state time and place, please, and I'll speed off into the night."

Alicia clicked an efficient nod. "Very well, Jeff. I will be delighted to see you again at eleven o'clock in the morning at Viscount Tower. We can have a coffee together."

Apple had no need to use the key given him by Angus Watkin. The door of Buckingham Palace drew inwards as he neared it. The opener was a man who said, "Evening, One. Call me Bert. Come on in. Hungry?"

"Evening. Okay. Thanks. Yes."

"Got a bit of stew going. See, I didn't know if I'd be waiting for hours or not."

"I'm here for the night now," Apple said, going in.

"Or if you'd be alone or not. That's why I was here on the watch."

"All alone." Apple followed to the kitchen. "The next chapter opens at eleven in the morning." He was feeling pleased with himself, his triumph. Furthermore, he had been successful at laughing off his response to the disillusioned, disappointed way he had been stared at by the ASFC fan with spectacles.

"Sit down," Bert said. "Be ready in a jiffy." He was of medium build, sixty years old, wearing a baggy suit and tired shoes. Topped by pate baldness, his face had the cheery-battered look of an overpaid sparring partner.

While they were eating in the breakfast nook, following general talk, Apple asked, "Do you look after the house, Bert?"

"No, I'm visiting for just this job. We'll get started as soon as we've eaten."

"Started on what?"

Bert said, "Your instruction, One."

"Ah, so you're the expert in sex."

"You knew? Do I look it? Finish that stew. Is it a mite salty for your taste? Have some more bread."

Apple said, "Yes. No. Certainly. Not at all. Thanks."

There came the sound of a telephone ringing. Bert giving a not-my-business shrug, Apple got up and went to the living room. While picking up the receiver, he noted that his mother's water-colour had gone. It and anything else bearing the Porter name would have been removed, he realised.

The caller was Angus Watkin, who asked for a report with as much passion as though he wanted to know what the weather was like. Trying not to drawl, Apple told of his success.

Watkin said, "Well, if you couldn't date the young lady for this evening, Porter, you couldn't. One must be philosophical. Your new documents are in the hat-stand drawer. Good night." The line died.

Putting down the receiver in a philosophical mood about the putridness of his Control, Apple went along the hall and collected a wallet. It held all the usual papers, from driving licence to credit card, as well as accreditation from the non-existent West Danglington *Weekly Crier*. Everything, wallet included, had been rendered real-looking with handling and creasing.

In the kitchen Bert was at the sink. He said, "Eat up. Was that Wily Watkin? Get your stuff? I can fix coffee, if you want some."

"Had enough. Yes. Yes. Okay."

Over coffee Apple tried with subtle probing to learn something of the background of this man who looked an expert in sex the way Apple looked stunted. He got nowhere, which secretly satisfied him: the mystery stayed intact.

They went upstairs, Bert leading at a ploughman plod. Through the master-bedroom doorway, in the soft lighting and the warmth, Apple suddenly stopped. He went rigid.

On the bed was a woman.

Bert laughed deep in his throat.

The woman, her dark hair spread across the pillow, lay on her back with arms stretched aside and one leg with the knee up. She was naked except for long stockings and a suspender-belt, briefs and a bra, and a small eye-mask. Each item was black.

Bert gave another laugh. "Looks real, don't she?"

Apple nodded slackly and let his sinews take it midway easy. "I'll say. I was fooled there for a moment."

"Yes, our Shirl usually gets 'em."

"But I'm not expected to—um—?"

Bert shook his head in little dithers. "No no, nothing like that. Shirl's respectable."

Apple relaxed fully. Moving on to the foot of the bed, he had a good look at the dummy. He said, "A beautiful job."

"That she is."

"But tell me, why do we men find suspender-belts arousing?"

"Because," Bert said, "suchlike trimmings are the thin end of the wedge of bondage. And bondage is power, which we all secretly crave."

Pleased to realize that he was feeling vaguely twisted, or anyway a little base, Apple said, "Just so."

"Another thin ender," Bert said, "is that pinch of the cheek or slap on the bottom. It's the beginning of sadism, which again is power, which again we all want."

Apple was unaware that his top lip took on a slight, cruel curl as he said a languid "Precisely."

"But it's physiology we're interested in at the moment, not that other stuff, even though it is important in the stage-setting."

"Wine and soft music," Apple murmured as though he'd had endless experience in these matters.

"Atmosphere," Bert said, taking up a position at one side of the bed. "That's the best aphrodisiac."

"I find that myself."

"But a drop of bubbly never hurt. Stand over there, please. Not nervous, are you? Warm in here. Did you ever try martinis?"

Apple stood at the bed's other side. "Quite. Righto. No way. It is. Often."

Bert said, "To tell you the truth, One, it's the power of suggestion that counts. Give someone water and tell him it's a powerful aphrodisiac—he'll respond accordingly." He pointed to the dummy. "But to Shirl."

"To the beautiful Shirl."

"We'll begin with the pulse of the wrist, I think. Ready?"

"Carry on, Bert," Apple said urbanely.

For a while the lesson went well. Apple learned the SV (Sensuality Value) of places he hadn't been aware of in that connexion: the front of the wrist, the left side of the navel, a certain spot just below the shoulder-blades, the inner elbow, and the calf's uppermost plane. He learned how, for PE (Prime Effect), to blow on the wrist at whistle pressure; to nudge the navel-side with the thumb; to tap but never stroke under the shoulder-blades; to press the elbow front with that hollow between one's bottom lip and chin; to scrape gently over the calf with the finger-nails. It was all most instructive.

Only when Bert started in on the more bandied-about erogenous zones did Apple feel the stirrings of embarrassment. At once he sent three-quarters of his attention inwards. In the desert, while the helicopter roared urgently, he struggled sweating and fearful to escape his collapsed tent. The warmth of the bedroom was a distinct help.

Apple's remaining outbound awareness he shared among gauging the intensity of the pinkness on his face; trying to give correct replies to Bert's job-lots of statement and question, which he on purpose heard indistinctly; and recalling while it was still hot that moment on the threshold when he had frozen. The last got most cerebral voltage. Apple suspected mistily that Shirl's classic pose was the closest he would ever get in his spy career to seeing the genuine article.

All in all, it was a harrowing lesson. But a useful one, Apple allowed. He knew he would never forget about wrists, navels, shoulder-blades, elbows and calves.

While Bert put back on Shirl the garments he had removed, and then returned her to wherever it was above

that she rested between engagements, Apple waited downstairs. Bert came below, chatted for a spell still in his bedside manner, shook hands and left.

Liking the older man, Apple thought it drear that, all
things being as unequal as they were in the spy game, he
and Bert would probably never meet again, except perhaps by chance. Someday they might see each other on,
say, Oxford Street. In which case they would exchange
glances with the deadness of rival heirs at the lawyer's. It
wasn't simply that acquaintanceship was discouraged, and
it was; you never knew what the other man was up to and
who may be watching him.

Alone, Apple felt restless, which he found understand-
able. He was, after all, on a mission, he protested. Even if
he did have no intentions of seeing it come to fruition, it
was still a kosher caper.

So what he should do at least, he mused, was go out for a
drink before the pubs closed. He could stand at one end of
the bar and look mysterious.

Putting on a topcoat, he turned its collar up as he left
the house. He was glad, he told himself, that his
trenchcoat was down at the cottage. That would have
been too much. He was really glad.

It was a fine night. For two pins Apple would have
walked all the way to Bloomsbury, with the excuse of col-
lecting Ethel. But it wouldn't do to leave her out in the
night air. She had enough of that on weekends.

The pub Apple went into was picturesquely crowded
and noisy. Those people who weren't talking above the
television set were making themselves heard despite the
yammer from a bellicose pianist. It was a standard close-
to-closing scene, with enough smoke to start a dozen
rumours.

At the bar's middle stretch Apple got served with a
sherry on the rocks. After lighting a cigarette in self-de-

fence, he had a more lingering look around. He noted that several of the younger women present had a flashiness, a hardness but also a bright brashness, that suggested they could be professionals in the business of sex.

That, coupled with his recent experience, started Apple on mental nods. Gradually he saw what could be a career-saver when he "failed" in this seduction caper.

He could hire a prostitute, his thoughts bubbled. She would only need to be roughly the right height and build. Her hair she would hide under a scarf, most of her face under a mask. Why would Angus Watkin suspect that she was not Alicia Suvov? The prostitute, well paid, would be told by her client that he was kinky, that he got his jollies out of frustration. After she had undressed except for the mask and scarf, he wanted her to speak for the first time since the door had been bolted. She had to shout "No!"— then pick up her clothes and run out.

Angus Watkin, Apple mused, would be told that although his underling, through a sheer wizardry of sexual magnetism plus spycraft, had managed to get the subject into the correct place and the desired mood, her puritanism had rebelled at the last stitch, as the cameras showed. The lady, in fine, was beyond seduction.

Apple liked it. He thought that even if the gambit didn't work, in the sense of being believed, at least it would commend him to Watkin for his richness of deceit.

Cheery, Apple moved to the end of the bar to look mysterious.

In Viscount Tower's lobby there were four of the Seven Dwarfs among the throng. This Apple learned with casual sweeps of his vision as he swung arcs on his stool, which he had been lucky to get: the coffee shop was doing brisk trade for the mid-morning break.

In respect of Dwarfs, Apple further noted that on hand

were what could be replacements for the missing originals. They had the required appearance of being nobody
special as well as making the giveaway point of looking
neither at each other nor at the possible competition who
was sitting tall at the counter.

Apple amused himself by trying to pick out which of
the originals was Angus Watkin's caper-watcher. It was
difficult, the men looking equally sinister.

At ten minutes past eleven (an acceptable female late-
ness, Apple felt), Alicia and Babushka came down the
stairs. The latter split off to head for the newsstand, Alicia
came towards the coffee-shop area.

She was wearing a modified but striking version of a
Cossack outfit: loose blouse, pants and mid-high boots, the
colours silver through red to black. As if to soften the bold
effect, she had her hair pulled severely back like a third-
generation teacher's grandmother.

Apple flicked his gaze around as he got up. Three of the
Dwarfs had their eyes on the chess star. The eyes of the
fourth met fleetingly those of Apple, who thought, Know
any good Angus Watkin jokes?

Alicia said as she arrived, in Russian, "I hope you
haven't been waiting long."

Apple almost answered in the same language, his mouth
and tongue working up to forming the first word, but his
voice-box caught itself in time.

"If that's an apology for being late," he said, "forget it.
By Western standards you're fifteen minutes early."

In English: "Thank you. And please excuse my forget-
fulness in using Russian."

"It's hardly surprising in that outfit you've got on. You
look terrific."

"Careful, Jeff," Alicia laughed. "I'm not used to that
kind of compliment."

"You're not?"

"People generally reserve their flattery for my skill at playing chess."

Rather than attempt to produce something even more gallant, which, he knew, he was capable of getting backwards or left-handed, at least, Apple contented himself with offering his seat with a bow. During it, he enjoyed a sly ogle of Alicia's inner wrist.

She suggested, "Or we could have a short stroll outdoors."

Not caring for the outside region thereabouts (he had approached warily), Apple said, "It's chilly today."

"Then let us stand," Alicia said. "I like standing beside tall men."

Wondering if he had just passed some sort of test, Apple got coffees. The following conversation about height, which he'd had four million times, he steered by degrees onto Alicia's schedule for today.

It was busy, apparently, but ended at nine o'clock. "That is when I am free to wash my hair at last."

"Be nice if you could do it some other time," Apple said. "Then we could have dinner together." He hurried on to tell of this little old English restaurant he knew of, well aware that the hardest type of cooking to find in London was British.

Alicia looked interested, even though she asked, "Would you want me to have dirty hair?"

"Your hair would still be beautiful in any condition," Apple said. He spoke naturally. He wasn't thinking compliments. He was stating his opinion.

Alicia ticked off three blinks and asked a stark "What time?"

"What time what?"

"Dinner tonight."

"Well—um—nine o'clock," Apple said. He went on to

explain where the Lichfield Grill and Chop House could be found, in Soho. "But I'll pick you up."

Alicia said, "No, best to meet there. Best away from here, as before."

"I'll be waiting at the restaurant," Apple said in all-round soggy relief. "But to get back to the benefits of being tall as opposed to . . ."

For a while longer they talked, with Alicia saying every few minutes that she had to go at once. Finally she did go, following a lingering handshake and more of that eye business, a primitive form of language with which Apple was less successful than with the verbal variety.

After Alicia, trailed by Babushka, had gone out of sight up the stairs, Apple turned away. He was almost at the exit when a man slid into his path like a religious maniac selling magazines and said, "Excuse me, but aren't you . . . ?"

"No," Apple said, circling, "I certainly am not." He went on to the door and outside. The man had been a Dwarf.

With a glance behind to check that he wasn't being followed, Apple set off across the forecourt alertly. He reached the pavement and looked about in order to remember which direction led to the safely-distant spot where he had left Ethel.

Not again, was his first fast thought when a growling erupted. He swung around. But it wasn't a motor-cycle. It was a black dog, a German shepherd the size of a donkey. And it was bounding straight at Agent One.

Who had about three seconds left to decide what to do. He did know a couple of sure-fire methods of dealing with this situation, which, obviously, was not born of accident. He had learned them in Training Five.

But fear of the snarling jaws made his mind go blank. He stood on in a stoop of indecision, like a man who wonders if he should go back inside and apologise, until the dog began its leap. Then he jumped aside.

In front of him was a kerb-parked car. Noting vaguely that it was a Rolls-Royce, he stretched his long legs high to make another jump, up onto the car's front. Standing there like a mouse-hounded woman on a chair, he turned. As he did, he heard from inside the car a roar of anger.

Stooping, Apple looked in a polite manner through the windshield. A red-faced man with an RAF moustache was gaping up in astonishment and outrage.

Apple looked away as the black dog came back. It tried to jump up to attack, but was thwarted from getting all the way by having Apple's foot jabbed in its face. It struggled to stay on the fender, claws scrabbling on paintwork.

From inside the car came a scream of pain, from somewhere near at hand came a whistle. The dog sped away and the livid driver opened his door to get out.

Not caring to hang around, plus bearing non-involvement in mind, Apple took a far-flying leap off the car and onto the roadway. Recovered from his landing, he started to run, chased by shrill pipings of agony.

The reason Apple went to Bloomsbury instead of Buckingham Palace was mainly because he wanted to start a fresh expense sheet for the mission, though he told himself it was to get his new pink shirt.

While garaging Ethel, he finally allowed himself to think of the Rolls-Royce, yet only insofar as to acknowledge that its owner must surely carry fully comprehensive insurance. As for causation, the well-trained assault dog, Apple wished, A, that he'd had the presence of mind to try out on it commands in different languages to see which one it responded to and, B, that he had received at least a small bite as another caper wound.

In his apartment Apple typed a new list of expenses.

This one included the to-and-fro Hampstead taxicab rides of last night and today's two coffees. He tutted at himself for not stopping on the way here for lunch, but recalled that he would be dining this evening at the Lichfield Grill and Chop House, which was gratifyingly expensive.

While eating a banana sandwich (the fruit mashed up with milk and sugar before being spread), Apple planned his afternoon. He would prepare a small photograph album with selected pictures. He would have a siesta. He would think up fascinating things to say to Alicia. He would shower and change. He would walk the stone's throw to Soho to pass time. He would call in and report his continuing success at maintaining his relationship with the subject. That first.

Whistling airily between his teeth after their post-lunch cleaning, Apple went to the telephone. As always, he enjoyed the rigmorole of getting connected with Upstairs and then with Angus Watkin. He refused to be deflated when his Control opened with "I have tried to contact you at Buckingham Palace, Porter."

Apple explained about the photograph album before saying, crisply, "Subject and I have an engagement for dinner."

"Let's hope it develops in the right direction."

"Yes, sir. Let us."

"And by the way, Porter," Angus Watkin said, "if it does, do make sure that the lady's face is free of impediments, won't you. Good afternoon."

Apple sighed.

The Lichfield Grill and Chop House was closed. Its Greek owners were sick, the chef had returned to Holland and the Spanish waiters were on strike. This information came from a youth who stood in a Soho slouch near the door, and who then went on to offer to supply a woman, hashish or the clean version of Fanny Hill.

Refusing to despond at that, or at the restaurant's closure, Apple asked the youth where he recommended dining. The youth asked what it was worth. Apple gave up.

He walked back to the corner, reaching it just as a taxi stopped there with Alicia. Greetings over, cab gone, they discussed the matter of food and decided to take a chance on the first place they came across, if it looked reasonably clean.

"I adore risks," Alicia said. Her Cossack outfit was topped by a hip-length cape. "Apart from with chess, there are so few of them in my life."

"In mine too," Apple said, thrilled to be lying. "Though I did get attacked by a mad dog outside Viscount Tower." He mentioned the incident and went on to give details as they walked the lamplit street, their elbows sometimes suggestively touching, because, he supposed, Alicia might hear of it and wonder why she hadn't been told about it by the near-victim himself.

The first restaurant was a hundred metres distant. They reached it just as Apple was about to think, Here I am, strolling through narrow, dimly lit, sinister streets with a foreign beauty.

Tied to no particular nationality, the restaurant seemed clean and mundanely acceptable. There was a lit candle on every table. Apple opened the door.

When they were seated, engrossed in their menus, Alicia said, "What have you been doing today, Jeff? The leek soup sounds very interesting."

"Working hard," Apple said, with a nod to show sincerity. "So does the bean." He gave no nods while telling of the piece on luxury automobiles he was writing for the West Danglington *Weekly Crier*.

"And what is that book you have with you?"

The photographs kept them busy until a waiter came. They ordered samely: leek soup followed by chicken à la king followed by cheese. The waiter asked about wine.

Alicia shook her head. "I shall not have any tonight, thank you, Jeff."

"Nor I," Apple said. He asked for the water list.

After handing it over, the waiter mumbled a bored-sounding "May I suggest the Perrier Blue, sir?" The inference was that any name would do, since most people didn't know one water from another.

Apple looked up from the card, slowly. Features and voice dead, he said, "The Blue is a shade savage, in my opinion."

The waiter winced. "Yes, sir," he whispered. "Sorry."

Apple scanned the list again, a forefinger pressed to the tip of his nose, the while asking Alicia if she had any preferences. The choice she would leave to him, she said.

He looked up at the waiter, his eyes slender. "How's the Welsh Stream?"

"Very good, sir," the man said. He stooped a little lower. "And I think, sir, that I can find you a February."

"Excellent," Apple said at once, returning the card with a flourish. "Carry on." For his cavalier attitude he forgave himself, the waiter being younger by far, but he knew all the same that he was going to leave a twenty per cent tip.

When the bottle of Welsh Stream came, Apple poured some for Alicia and told her he believed she would find it an amusing little water. Alicia said she adored men who knew about such things.

Apple was still trying to recall other such things, fretfully, when the first course arrived.

As the meal progressed, Apple relaxed as much as Alicia appeared to be relaxing. He became simply a man having dinner with an alluring woman. Once, making a conversational point, he touched her left wrist (the outer side).

Twice Alicia patted his hand. Several times their gazes got so active and eloquent that Apple's right eye grew over-moist.

Later, stirring her coffee, Alicia said, "It was a fine meal, Jeff. Thank you."

"Entirely my pleasure, m'dear," Apple murmured, bold in his comfort.

"Tomorrow it will be my turn. I want you to come and have lunch with me."

Grandly, Apple said, "I'll be delighted, Alicia. Many thanks." It was all so easy, he told himself in a thrum, if a man knew what he was about.

"One o'clock at Viscount Tower?"

"That will suit me nicely."

After giving him the telephone code-number of her suite, Alicia said, "I shall reserve a table for three in the hotel restaurant."

Less grandly: "Ah yes, your companion."

"Oh no, not Irini. She rarely joins me on social outings of this nature. But did I forget to mention it?"

"Mention what?"

"My boy-friend. He is arriving tomorrow. He will be having lunch with us."

The rest of Apple's grandness backed away like a duke from the monarch. His upper body tapped a similar re-treat until it was hard against the chair. His mind tried for an urbane response and came up with "Eh?"

"My boy-friend," Alicia said pleasantly. "Edward Baker. He is arriving on the Concorde tomorrow morning from New York."

"Oh. I see."

"If he shows up, he will be lunching with us."

"He might not? Show up?"

"I do not know how reliable he is," Alicia said. "Could I have a cigarette, please?"

Apple put the two cigarettes into burning service with no more than six fumbles. He was counting in order to get his worries in sequence and ignore a sear of jealousy.

He said, "Sounds to me as though you don't know this man very well."

"As a matter of fact, Jeff," Alicia said, patting his hand by way of thanks for the cigarette, "I do not suppose I know him much better than I know you."

"Curious name," Apple mused aloud with frost, "Edward Baker."

"Perhaps I should not use the term boy-friend. It means something stronger in English, I think."

"How long have you known this Baker person?"

Smiling, Alicia told of three or four dates last month during a Chicago chess tournament. "Then I saw him briefly in New York on my way here."

"You must like him."

"I imagine so. Edward is amusing. It would be nice if I could meet him at the airport, but I have an engagement."

Trying for the casual touch, Apple asked, "How did you two meet in the first place?"

"At a reception," Alicia said. She drew on her cigarette luxuriously, spreading the smoke. "Though I found out afterwards that he, as the saying goes, was crashing. Edward is like that, you see."

"Is he really?" Apple prickled.

"Yes. Very much so."

Apple asked further questions, growing outwardly more casual as inwardly he became more tense; as it began to sink in that he had a real problem on his hands. Edward Baker represented danger in more ways than one.

To start with, Apple thought, this Baker character could bring about the caper's demise, through the subject spending most of her time with him instead of with Agent One. Next, Baker could easily be an espionage operative (CIA

or almost any other) who was working towards the same
sex-film entrapment, from which Alicia had to be pro-
tected at whatever cost. Last, Edward Baker was a rival for
the attentions of somebody whom Agent One had grown
to like more than just slightly.

The situation, Apple recognised, was plus-serious. Every answer of Alicia's highlighted that fact: Edward Baker
was tall, good-looking and with dark wavy hair, a Yale
graduate, a fair chess player, a rich man's son who didn't
have to work for a living, an amateur poet who was at-
tracted to anarchy, skilled as a pilot, skier and driver of
racing cars.

Stubbing out his cigarette, Apple said drily, "Sounds
like a matinee idol."

"Mmm," Alicia said. "But I still have my hair to wash.
If the waiter could get me a taxi . . ."

Ten minutes later, after being given a short, plump kiss
on the lips by Alicia, Apple was watching her taxicab
draw away. When it had turned out of sight, he began to
walk.

He went slowly, head down, the photograph album flat
to his chest within his folded arms. He needed to think
carefully about the elimination from the scene of Edward
Baker—to be brought off by Agent One, who would
rather grow an inch taller than ask Angus Watkin for help.

Since a relationship already existed between Alicia and
the American, Apple mused, there was no sense in trying
ploys with motor-cycles, ladders or dogs. The situation
called for something truly Machiavellian. Even, you might
say, evil.

FOUR

The timing, at least, would be neat, Apple thought as he followed arrows at Heathrow airport. He would have a good hour in hand afterwards to get to his lunch date. Also it had been phone-call simple to discover the arrival time of today's Concorde from New York. Nor had there been too many difficulties in making arrangements at Lilac Grange, where money spoke as loudly as it did at any other borderline establishment.

Apple steered into a multi-storey car park. No, he mused, there was only one aspect of the plan that could be a spanner, and that was Edward bloody Baker himself. Everything depended on his gullibility, at least to begin with.

Parking the rented black Ford, Apple locked it and headed for the terminal building. He yawned, in part because of nerves, in part because of tiredness. The plan could be as successful as green milk; last night, retiring late after much ignoring of the telephone call-signal, he had slept badly, often struggling awake to escape dreams of being clawed by German shepherds.

A vast board that looked like a refugee from the stock exchange told him that the Concorde was five minutes early. Apple yawned again. He was always nervous of good omens like that.

Apple stood behind the throng near the door of Arrivals. He would have paced if it hadn't been that so many

others were pacing; he had no wish to be one of the sheep-
herd save in respect of height.

Passengers began coming through, some shoving lug-
gage-laden carts. Soon appeared a tall man with wavy hair
whose clothes were so expensive they looked off-the-peg.
His nationality was stated by the parched skin that central
heating gives Americans, as though as a penalty for them
preferring comfort over cold backs and spine-straighten-
ing bedrooms.

Bent on interception, Apple strode around the throng.
When he had almost reached his goal, the tall man sud-
denly dropped his two suitcases and shouted, "Darling!"
He and an attractive woman embraced.

Sheering off, Apple circled. He was in time to see another man of the same ilk going outdoors and carrying one
small flight bag. Apple used long, jittery strides to catch
up, calling as he neared, "Mr. Edward Baker?"

The man stopped, turned. "That's right."

He was so good-looking that Apple's voice took on a
snap for "I'm Inspector Carter of the Special Branch."

Casually, confidently: "The special what?"

"It's the department of Scotland Yard that deals with
espionage, Mr. Baker. I'm here to meet you on behalf of
Miss Alicia Suvov."

Baker tilted back his head for a more thorough ap-
praisal. He asked, "And just what has Alicia got to do with
espionage?"

"I'll explain as we drive," Apple said. He remembered
to sound urgent. "There's no time to be lost. This way,
please." He went on talking of haste and secrecy and, in a
vague manner, of danger, as he brisked the way across to
the car park. When Edward Baker asked to see his identification, he pretended not to hear.

They got in the car. Driving off, Apple said, "We'll be
there in fifteen minutes. Don't worry."

"I have no intentions of worrying. I guess if I stick around long enough, you'll tell me what the hell's going on."

Apple threw him a glare. Harshly he said, "I don't believe, Mr. Baker, that you've heard a word I've told you."

"Well, I—"

"You *are* Edward Baker of Chicago, aren't you?"

"Sure I am," the passenger said, reaching for a pocket. "I can prove it."

"Never mind," Apple snapped. "Of course you're Baker. I know because you've been watched ever since you checked in for your flight early this morning."

"Why, for God's sake? But talking of identification . . ."

"We were talking, Baker, of Miss Suvov, whom we are on our way to see."

"Oh we are, eh? Good."

Apple let out a short, sharp sigh, like a husband who wouldn't dream of complaining. "I knew it," he said. "You haven't been listening."

"Well, I don't know about that."

"Perhaps you don't want to help Miss Suvov. Is that it?"

Edward Baker became sincere. He rounded his back in apology and explanation. Of course he wanted to help Alicia. She was a great kid. He was crazy about her. It was just that he didn't understand what was going on here, for God's sake.

Less chill, Apple raised a hand: "Yes yes."

"And another thing is, I have jet-lag. I'm not really at my brightest."

"What you need, Baker, is a drink."

"Yes, I do. I sure do. That's what I need."

"There's a pub around the next bend."

"Do we have time?"

"We can fit it in. We have to. Miss Suvov, I know, will want to see you looking calm and in control of yourself."

With a pale whine of exasperation, Edward Baker asked, "But what is all this about?"

"Wait. Let's get that drink."

The pub, set beside a traffic roundabout as though to catch spin-offs, had more slot machines than customers at this early hour. Smiling a welcome was a barmaid who wore enough cosmetics to serve a duo clown act.

"Two double whiskies," Apple told her. He ignored Baker's mumble that he liked rye himself.

The drinks came. Apple, acting haste, quickly lifted a glass and turned towards his companion as if to speak. They bumped—and most of the whisky went onto Baker's lapel.

In the following confusion of mop-up and regrets, Apple managed to spread the dampness and order two more doubles. These they sipped in the aftercalm, Baker looking abused as well as mystified. The first, surviving drink Apple divided between the new ones, making sure that the other man got most.

Whether or not Edward Baker was an espionage agent, Apple didn't know. He easily could be. At the moment it mattered only insofar as he might, should he have an operative's training, see straight through this ploy of getting him to smell drunk and—Apple hoped—look it if not actually be it (and his jet-lag eyes did have a nice redness); he might also later be able to extricate himself one way or another from confinement.

At Lilac Grange, a private clinic, one of those places which bitterly regret the legalization of abortion, staff were expecting nice tall Mr. Brown to bring his friend along for the standard three-day, pre-paid, all-inclusive session of drying out done the easy way: under sedation. It had been a treat, staff thought, to see how particular Mr.

Brown was about the clinic's security arrangements, so concerned was he for the safety of his dipsomaniac friend, who tended to try to run away when called by one of his drink-wrought delusions.

But Edward Baker was sipping slowly. As an encouragement, Apple drained his glass. Being unused to spirits, he gagged. With effort he was able to turn the act into a bout of realistic coughing.

He wheezed out at the barmaid, who was patting her chest in sympathy, "Two more doubles, please."

"Well now," the American said. "You were going to explain this business, Mr.—?"

"Cartwright," Apple said huskily.

"And you're a regular policeman?"

"Chief Inspector, Special Branch."

"If Alicia's in some kind of heavy trouble, you might as well get it out."

With his fresh drink Apple made little lurches towards his mouth, inviting imitation. He said, "I'm not sure if I should tell you, not without clearance."

Baker obliged with a spinster sip. "On what?"

"On you. From the Federal Bureau of Investigation."

"You've got to be kidding."

Apple straightened his shoulders. "I am not the type to jest about national security."

Looking as though he had belched during the saying of grace, Edward Baker raised the glass towards his lips, at which point Apple jogged the up-moving arm. Baker received a fair splash of whisky over his tie and the lower half of his face.

Pretending not to have noticed, Apple asked the barmaid for the correct time. He was wondering how long all this was going to take. They didn't have all the time in the world, after all, he fretted.

Five minutes to twelve, the barmaid reported. Edward

Baker, stuffing a handkerchief back in his top pocket, asked, "Are we going to be late?"

Apple said no, the barmaid asked where they were going, Baker said he didn't know, Apple ordered more whisky, the barmaid said as she left that they were a couple of characters if you asked her.

"Let's get this straight," Edward Baker muttered like a lawyer out of court. "Is Alicia in trouble or not?"

"Yes," Apple said, "and no."

Heavily: "Thank you. I appreciate you laying it on the line."

"It all depends on certain matters."

"Well, how does espionage come into all this?"

"What makes you think it does?" Noticing that his glass was empty, Apple put it down and reached out towards the approaching barmaid, who handed him his fresh drink.

Edward Baker said, "Look, you definitely told me that espionage was involved here."

"Espionage?" the barmaid said. "That means spies and all that stuff."

Apple, feeling fine, leaned comfortably on the bar and began explaining that he and his friend were going to see a spy movie. Next, he went into the plot of the espionage novel he had been unable to put down last week.

At a tap on his shoulder, Apple looked around. Edward Baker said, "I hope I'm not interrupting anything, but I guess it's time we were on our way."

"When you've had a drink," Apple said like a hurt host. "You must have a drink, Edward."

"And then we'll go?"

"Go where?"

Baker's gaze moved to the wall, staying there until Apple said, "See, it's a secret."

"I thought it might be."

Apple ordered two double whiskies, finished the drink he was holding, jollied Baker into draining his glass, handed him another when the new drinks came. He said, "Shears."

"Cheers," Edward Baker said. "You don't seem as worried as you were, Inspector."

"Superintendent," Apple said, returning to a low-slung forearm lean. "Worried?"

"About getting to wherever it is we're going. At the airport you told me there was no time to be lost."

"Time," Apple said. "Yes. You've got something there." In starting to push himself up from the bar, he skidded on his elbow. On the next try he made it, the while laughing lightly to show that it was all nothing, nothing.

Baker said, "It seems to me that there was also some mention of danger."

Wondering if he could be a teensy bit tight, Apple stopped laughing in order to frown. "As I keep saying," he grated, "we have no time to lose. Knock that drink back and we'll be off. We can't stay here all day, you know."

The barmaid said what a shame, Baker said he didn't know if he could knock it back.

"Like this," Apple said. He lifted his head back, opened his mouth and tossed in the whisky. It tried to come out again at once. But Apple, appalled at the idea of being messy, creating a scene, fought to effect ingestion.

Watched with interest by Baker and the barmaid, he quivered all over himself like someone fighting the dry heaves, his arms on a loose dangle. He won, swallowing noisily. Through a false smile he gave wet gasps.

Edward Baker asked, "Like that?"

Apple was glad to see the gates of Lilac Grange, with a gravel driveway beyond. He had grown tired of his passenger offering him advice like a driving instructor, for one thing. For another, the rented car's steering was so bad that real effort and concentration were needed merely to keep from running into the side.

Now, Edward Baker gave yet another of his odd, croaky hisses: the Ford's side-view mirror had smacked against a gatepost. Apple snorted at how ill-placed the post was. For a pin or two he would complain when they got inside.

"Are we here?" Baker asked in a miniature voice.

"We are. It's been a long journey."

"Oh God."

Poor man was worried about Alicia being in trouble, Apple thought as he let the car have its way and run up onto the drive's grass verge. He came down again to turn the last bend, the house appearing.

Edward Baker whispered, "We can stop now. Be foolish to drive up the steps."

Apple brought the car to a grinding halt nose-in to the broad stone stairway. He got out with a snatch of song and told Baker not to forget his bag.

"What for? I'm not staying here."

"Just bring the bag, Ed. The lady will explain all."

"In for a penny," the passenger sighed, getting out.

Weaving around to the other side of the car, telling himself with amusement that yes, he was a teensy bit, weensy bit tight, Apple took hold of Baker's arm assistingly. They began to go up, Edward Baker straight of body and set of face, Apple lurching and grinning.

"Mind how you go, Eddy lad," he said, as well as, "You'll be all right."

They went inside. Reception, a hallway in invalid green, had two nurses and an intern. They rose from their comic books, smiled as though they meant it, clasped their hands like pawnbrokers.

"Hello, hello!" Apple called cheerily. "Here we are. Better never than late."

"Good day, Mr. Brown," staff unisoned. "And this must be Mr. Baker."

"That's right," Edward Baker said briskly. He pulled free of Apple, who then, anchorless, went off into a drifting walk. He circled a chair as smoothly as a skater and came back to the group as the intern was beaming:

"Time for us to have a little nap now, Mr. Baker."

The American nodded several times, his eyes peculiar. "You go right ahead, folks."

One nurse took his bag. The other began to reverse away from him, in a stoop, her hands out enticingly as if he were two going on three. She cooed, "This way, Mr. Baker."

Edward Baker looked everywhere he could reach without moving his head. He said, "Wait a minute."

Apple laughed, "I knew you were going to say that."

"Wait just a goddam minute here."

"I hope you're going to be good, Eddy lad."

"Am I crazy or something?" Edward Baker asked as he did a scan of faces.

The bag-holding nurse said, "No, dear—wrecked." She put her free hand on Baker's upper arm, behind the biceps, making him stiffen with a gasp.

Knowing the hold, Apple gave a jerk of sympathy. That caused him to lose his balance. However, by raising his arms sideways to the horizontal he managed to keep it together.

The nurse who was reversing to a doorway said, "Come on, Mr. Baker. You want to see Barbra, don't you?"

Baker, being eased firmly in that direction by the other nurse, asked a faint "Barbra? Who's Barbra?"

"Barbra Streisand, dear. Your girl-friend."

"No no. My girl-friend's Alicia Suvov, the chess player."

"Oh boy," the intern said.

Over his shoulder, Edward Baker whispered, "Inspector? Chief Superintendent? What's happening?"

Apple told the intern with an elaborate gesture, "Pathetic. Poor old Edders thinks I'm from Scotland Yard. It's terribly shad."

The American was muttering about all this being a horrible mistake, a confusion of identities, as he and his captor followed the reversing nurse out. The door closed with a snicker of finality.

Moving to a desk, the intern said, "Congratulations, Mr. Brown, on your act."

"Thank you," Apple said, not knowing what the man meant but deciding not to mention gateposts anyway.

"Not only because you do the act of being drunk very well, sir, but because you realised the need for it. You can't beat humouring 'em."

"Oh?"

"If you'll just sign here, please, Mr. Brown."

Apple reached the desk in three lurchy strides. Signing, handing over the rest of the fee, shaking the intern's hand —these actions he was aware of but foggily as he struggled to keep from slurring or swaying; and to absorb what the man had said.

Next, Apple was in the car telling himself: Drunk. Never mind the teensies and the weensies. Never mind tight. He was drunk. Smashed. Stonkered. Pissed to the gills. And he had to get to Little Venice, where he was expected to be suave, sober and charming.

With a groan Apple started the car. He reversed an arc, drove forwards and narrowed his eyes warningly at the grass verges. He safely reached the gateway. Passing through, he picked up speed until he was driving as fast as he considered prudent.

He soon realised, however, that he wasn't going to make

it in time, by a long way, if he stayed at nine miles an hour. The answer was to forget about being the driver.

Stopping in the next commercial district he came to, Apple parked the car and slooped off in search of a taxi.

When he saw the taxi-cab rank, he began to gather himself together. By the time he reached the first taxi, he was so rigid he could hardly move his arm to open the door. The driver reached back and did it for him.

During the drive, which he spent lying on his side on the seat, folded up like a praying mantis, Apple fondled his latest guilts in the abstract. He became lumpy of throat over scratched paintwork and innocent people being held prisoner against their wills.

The taxi stopped in front of Viscount Tower. Apple paid, took a solemn farewell of the cabbie and trundled across the forecourt with the small steps of an asthmatic geisha. On the threshold lay a thick doormat. Cunning, not risking a trip, Apple performed a sprightly leap.

As he was recovering from his landing, he saw Alicia. She was staring at him from near the reception desk, the clock above which said that Jeff Poor was ten minutes late.

Rigid again, Apple made his robot way across the lobby. Not until he was drawing close did he note the stolidity of Alicia's features as she watched his approach. Letting himself relax, he laughed and waved. Alicia closed her eyes briefly.

She said, when Apple came to an arm-dangling halt in front of her, "I am outraged."

"Aw come on, Alicia. Ten minutes is nothing. Traffic will be traffic, y'know."

"Please do not insult my intelligence. I am not talking about time."

"Well, if you think I've had a couple," Apple said, sniffing, "you're quite mistaken."

"The reason I am outraged," Alicia said in a measured scrape, "is at the lies and the masquerade."

Apple did an imitation of Edward Baker's eye-wander with unmoving head, at the same time becoming semi-rigid. "I don't know what you mean."

"I asked somebody at the Embassy to check for me. I liked you, you see. It was discovered, of course, that there is no such place as West Danglington, and certainly no such newspaper as the West Danglington *Weekly Crier*."

Apple said, "Ah."

"And no such person as Jeff Poor," Alicia said. After a heavy nod, she switched to Russian to continue, "As I suspected right from the start, comrade, you are a member of the KGB."

Loosening at the absurdity of it all, Apple said, also speaking Russian, "You're absolutely right, and you're absolutely wrong." He swayed with a snorty laugh.

Alicia's jaw firmed. "Don't bother to explain that dense remark. I haven't the time. I waited here simply to thank you for making a fool of me. Good-bye, comrade."

As she started to turn away, Apple grabbed her arm, saying, "Hold on a minute, Alicia. You're bounding to conclusions. Just because I'm not called Jeff Poor, that doesn't mean I'm KGB. I can assure you I am not."

"Naturally you would say that."

"Furthermore, I've never been to Russia in my life."

Alicia shook off his hand while turning back to face him. "So how can you speak Russian, and with no foreign accent?"

"I can explain with the greatest of ease."

"No doubt. You people can explain anything."

"Now let's get this straight," Apple said. "I'm a philologist. He hiccoughed. In French he told of his job, in German he described the United Kingdom Philological Institute, in Greek he apologised for the lies and masquerade, in Swedish he said it had all been to try to impress her, in Arabic he explained that he hadn't really known of her fame, in Italian he said he had seen her and decided that they had to meet.

"The rest you know," he said, returning to English.

In the same language Alicia said, "Most of that I got." Her face was less severe. "What was that about being impressed?"

Apple checked a sway. "I thought you'd be eager to be interviewed, you see, me not knowing that you were constantly under attack from reporters."

"It's a good story."

"I can prove all of it. All of it."

Leaning a fraction backwards, Alicia looked up at him carefully. "What's wrong with you? You seem different. Your eyes are red. Your hair is messy."

"I'm perfectly fine."

"There is something different about you," she insisted. "Those eyes."

Apple, who had already started flipping rapidly through the mental file-cards he had retained from Training Seven's lectures on appearances, which supplied explanations to cover everything from a limp to a bloody nose, chose "A motor-bike."

"I beg your pardon?"

"I've been riding a motor-cycle. Without goggles. No goggles on me, I mean." He laughed.

"Oh, you have a motor-cycle?"

"I borrowed a friend's," Apple said, dismissing that with a generous wave. "But to get back to me. Do you still think I'm with the KGB? Really? Honestly?"

Alicia waggled a hand like a fish. "More or less, yes. I do not know. I am easily swayed."

After sucking his forefinger, Apple made a sloppy diagram on his chest. "Cross my heart and hope to die, I'm not KGB."

"If you are, it is a shame. We had such nice times together, Jeff—or whatever your name is."

"It's Appleton Porter. That's what my name is. But please go on calling me Jeff. I like it."

"So do I."

"And if you'll bear with me for a while, Alicia, I can prove to you that I'm not what you think."

She folded her arms like an executioner. "How?"

"How? Yes, I see. How am I to convince you that I'm just an innocent philologist?"

"No doubt you'll think of something."

Apple tried to snap his fingers. They slithered. "I know," he said. "I'll take you to the Institute, my place of work. If, that is, you're willing to give me a chance."

"Right now? At once?"

"Absolutely."

"So you would have no time to set things up?"

"We leave right away."

"Very well," Alicia said. "To be just, I do owe you at least the opportunity."

Apple stooped an elaborate bow. "Many thank yous."

"I'll slip upstairs and get a coat."

"It's not cold out today."

Alicia raised her eyebrows. "But it will be cold on a motor-cycle, naturally." She turned away. "I will be back in three minutes. Do not move."

Watching her go towards the stairs, Apple blinked drably. Once again he had managed to out-clever himself, he thought. Now there was another lie that had to be dealt with—unless he could pull off a neat one.

Slurring a look around the assembly, Apple picked out the Dwarf whom he had figured might be a Brit, Angus Watkin's caper-watcher. But to go to him directly could be fatal. Alicia, or maybe Babushka, could be covertly observing to see what Poor-Porter would do now. If he acted in any way suspiciously, he would be forever condemned as a Hammer—male KGB agent—and held at the greatest of all possible distances. Alicia would then be open to entrapment by any of the other spook outfits.

Swallowing sentimentally therefore the idea that he was actually doing all this for Alicia, Apple got out a cigarette. He moved off and went to the closest person who was most unlikely to have a light, an older woman with a camelesque expression. With his eyebrows performing the question, he wafted the cigarette near his mouth. The woman shook her head coldly.

Apple moved on at a swift lurch, thinking, Three minutes. He did his routine in front of a teen-age girl, got a giggled head-shake and then headed for the assumed Brit, who, at the approach, skipped his eyes about nervously like a caught voyeur.

Halting, holding the cigarette high, Apple said with stiff lips, "You might just not know what I'm talking about, sport, but my name's One and I need a motor-bike within the next two minutes. It's an emergency."

The man, plain and mild-looking, said, "Sorry, I don't smoke myself."

Apple turned and walked off, throwing his cigarette away as if giving up on the idea. Glancing back a moment later, he saw that the man had gone. Apple didn't know what to think.

Near the desk he burped, grimaced, clopped his mouth. He was beginning to feel less drunk, which meant he was starting to feel the after-effects of the alcohol. At the moment he didn't much care what happened.

With bleak eyes and sagged mouth, he stared at the stairway, coming alert, messily, only when Alicia appeared. She wore an ankle-length suede coat.

Striding directly to Apple, she asked, "Are we still going on this trip?"

"Of course."

"You look as though you do not know what to do now that I have called your bluff. If bluff it was."

"It wasn't. We are definitely going to my work place. By cab if it's raining."

"The weather is perfectly dry," Alicia said. "Come on."

Mumbling that it looked as though it could pour down at any second, Apple followed lackey-like towards the door. There, with arms folded, stood the assumed Brit. One of his hands had its forefinger extended downwards: body-language for *Get close*.

In passing, Apple got close enough, and went slow enough, to hear "White Honda. To your right. Move off fast. I stole it."

"Thanks," Apple tossed back like a pinch of salt, after which he wondered, And if this guy's not really a Brit, will the bike be booby-trapped?

Catching up to Alicia, Apple took her to a large white motor-cycle standing with others at the forecourt's edge. That it was the right machine showed by a piece of plastic sticking out from where the key should be.

Pointing to the crash-helmet hung on the handlebar, Apple said, "There's only one. I'd forgotten about that."

"What does it matter?"

"By law in this country, helmets have to be worn by everyone." After being glad of the machine's availability, he was now glad of an out. He felt more like lying down than driving. "We'll take a cab."

"Nonsense, Jeff. In the event of difficulties I shall claim diplomatic immunity or something. You are not trying to get out of this, are you?"

"We can easily get a taxi."

"You might find something wrong with it. I am on to all the tricks, you see. I have been through this before."

"Let's go."

One minute later they were driving off, Apple's head feeling worse inside the helmet. In addition to that, he didn't know which he dreaded most, the bike's sudden collapse or its owner's angry shout. He did know he wasn't enjoying the proximity of Alicia or her arms around his waist.

Almost immediately, within a few hundred metres, Apple got the sensation that they were being followed. On fast reflection, he wasn't surprised. This was, after all, the first time he and Alicia had given anybody the chance to tail.

The Honda had no side-mirror and Apple couldn't see behind by turning his head because of both Alicia and the helmet. But he would have gambled on the fact of having a shadow, if not three. The idea gave him no joy. He wasn't up to such a situation on top of everything else. And he now had the further strife of trying to drive the bike in a sober-sensible manner.

Trouble was, Apple thought, even if he were feeling great he would still have problems getting rid of whomever was behind, because if he did it in pro style, which would be fairly easy on a motor-cycle, that would sell him irreversibly to Alicia as a Hammer.

Apple didn't want to lead the way to Kensington nor risk injury to self or Alicia by zealous shadowers, yet he could see no escape—not, that is, until his passenger spoke loudly under the helmet near his ear.

She asked, "Are you quite sure you are going *straight* to this place?"

Apple turned his head aside to say yes, he was taking

the normal route but he did know a short cut. He nodded at her, "Go that way."

Grateful for the gift, Apple became alert to possibilities. He soon saw what seemed to be a useable alley. It was narrow, cluttered, no good to a car and only just good enough for a motor-cycle. This Apple found out after swinging abruptly, at speed, off the street and into the alley's mouth.

They side-swiped a garbage can, knocked over a pile of cartons and narrowly missed a box of kittens. They ducked to get under a line of washing, swerved to avoid a pile of scrap metal and splashed through a pool of rainwater. They hit a bump.

The bike went up, came down. The crash-helmet came down also, onto the bridge of Apple's nose. He couldn't see. He was embraced by panic. He shot up both hands, shot one back down again to the handlebar, pushed at the helmet. It wouldn't move. Alicia yelled at him to look out. He flung his head back. Through the mini-gap thus created he saw the obstacle, a crate of bottles. With a wild swing he got around it, to where they hit another bump. The bike went up, came down. The crash-helmet went back into place; and the alley ended.

Apple drooped like a dying flower. As he steered onto a street, he revved the engine loudly so that his groan couldn't be heard. That he had foxed the shadows failed to make his groan less anguished.

In ten minutes they were arriving at the Institute, a former manor house in typical Edwardian design. Alicia admired it politely after they had left the motor-cycle between two parked cars.

"Thank you," Apple said. He wondered if police walkie-talkies were spitting out information on a stolen Honda. Straight away he decided not. He didn't need the suspense right now.

As they were going towards the entrance, Alicia said, "If I were you and with the KGB, I would have this arranged."

"I wouldn't have had time."

"Yes you would. By telephone, while I was getting my coat. You could have arranged for people to be here, at this building, one that you do not even know very well. They would greet you. Hello, Mr. Porter, and so forth."

"Impossible to fix in only a few minutes," Apple said, safe in this at least. "After you."

As they went into the marble-decked hallway with its staircase curving up as voluptuously as an Edwardian female torso, a secretary came striding past. She hadn't spoken to Apple in nine years, not since he had singed her fringe while trying to light her cigarette in style.

She said, "Good day, Mr. Porter."

"Ah," Apple said.

"Lovely day."

"Yes." He kept his eyes on the secretary, who went on and began trotting upstairs, so he wouldn't see what kind of expression Alicia had produced.

He asked divertingly as they themselves started up the staircase, "What's going to happen with your friend? Edward Baker, was that the name? We'll keep him waiting for lunch."

"He won't be waiting."

"Why not?"

Alicia stopped on the next step. She looked up at Apple as he too stopped. "He did not appear," she said. "Which is somewhat curious, don't you think?"

Not cheered by knowing that if it weren't for the alcohol, he would now blush, probably, Apple said, "But you said yourself that he might not show up."

"That is true."

"And it might not have been him, his fault. His plane could have been delayed."

"True again." They went on up.

Above, three male researchers appeared. They came down one behind the other and, as they passed, instead of giving their usual off-hand nods, each bowed head and shoulders and said, "Hello, Porter."

Apple thought he could be losing his mind. At this moment, the possibility had a certain attraction.

At the top they turned onto a corridor, off which opened the doors of section-wall offices. By the time Apple and Alicia were midway along, almost every door had opened and the occupant had looked out with a greeting, the same coming from those people who walked past—and there seemed to be an unusually large number of people on the move here today. Apple had never heard his last name pronounced so often in such a short space of time.

"This is ridiculous," he said, leading the way into his own cramped office. "Why is everyone saying hello to me?"

Alicia looked amused. "Perhaps it is because you still have your crash-helmet on."

"Oh," Apple said. Then he realised that, of course, everyone was acting this way because of the presence of the celebrated lady chess player, word having spread from the singe secretary. He said so.

With a shrug Alicia said, "Anyway, if this is a set-up, it is very efficient."

"Thank you. I mean, no, of course it isn't."

"Perhaps just a *tiny* bit overdone."

"Let's go and see my chief."

At the corridor's end Apple knocked on a door and took Alicia into the office of Professor Warden. A crumpled man with white hair who spoke fourteen languages and was absent-minded in the expected professorial way, he was standing by his mess of a desk as if he wondered what it was doing there.

He stared at Apple. "Who are you?"

Apple quickly took off his helmet. "Me, sir."

"So you are. Good day to you—um—"

"Porter, sir."

"Precisely. I was just going to say that."

"I know you were, sir."

"And are you better now, my boy?"

After mumbling around that, Apple made the introduction. Professor Warden was visibly impressed. Speaking Russian, he expressed his delight at meeting the estimable Miss Suvov, shook both her hands, asked for her autograph, sat her in his chair at the desk and offered her the remains of a biscuit.

Alicia responded beautifully. Apple would have felt proud of them both, he thought, if he hadn't felt so rotten.

Biscuit finished, Alicia began to ask questions about junior colleague Porter. The answers seemed evasive because, as Apple knew and tried to convey to Alicia with smiles and formless signs, the professor couldn't remember how long Porter had worked at the Institute or what his job entailed exactly or if he attended every day at regular hours.

When Professor Warden briskly changed the subject, Apple got Alicia away. While they were on their way out, there were more greetings from colleagues—and Apple knew, without giving a Biblical-sense at the moment, that his stock had gone up several points at the United Kingdom Philological Institute.

In the street he asked, "Satisfied?"

"Perhaps," Alicia said. She took the crash-helmet from him. "Let us have a little ride, shall we? This time you can be the passenger."

Apple was so unenthusiastic about this development, so brimming with low spirits as well as concerned over the motor-cycle theft, to mention nothing of now being assailed by inklings of a hangover headache, that it wasn't until he was settling himself on the pillion seat behind Alicia, who had just started the engine with an expert kick, that he noticed the crash-helmet.

Shouting to be heard above the engine's racket, he said, "You've got the helmet on backwards."

Revving, Alicia turned her head to the side. "I know."

"You do?"

"Of course. I am not without motor-cycling experience."

Apple said, "But you won't be able to see."

"Right," Alicia said. "I got the idea from you on your short cut." She tapped the front of the helmet, where it touched the bridge of her nose. "I can see two metres of road beyond the front wheel."

"Well, just so long as you go at a crawl."

"But we are not going to be crawling," Alicia said lightly. "Quite the reverse."

Apple, alarmed, asked, "What d'you mean?"

The motor-cycle supplied the answer. It shot out of the parking spot and onto the road like a racehorse leaving the starting-gate. If he hadn't made a fast grab for the driver's waist, Apple would have fallen off backwards. As it was, he merely suffered a whiplash that made his neck scream and his headache come fully to life.

Moaning, he gathered his awareness together like a shredded cloak and realised that they were building up to a healthy speed. This abnegated any pleasure he might still have earned from having his arms around Alicia.

He shouted, "Slow down!"

"Sorry, Jeff," she said.

"But you can't see where you're going."

"I know. You have to give me directions. Our safety depends on you. You are my eyes."

Apple blurted, "This is ridiculous."

"Not at all," Alicia said. "You must tell me what to do."

"Okay. Stop dead and let me off."

"I can not do that, Jeff. This is the last test."

"Test of what?"

"Of you. If you pass it, I can trust you."

"If I—" Apple began, then changed to a screech of warning: they were aiming straight for the back of a stationary bus.

Alicia asked, "What's wrong?"

In hoarse gasps Apple gave directions. Bear right. Slow down. Go left a little. Alicia reacted well, though she slowed hardly at all. They went alongside the double-decker in safety.

Apple panted, "That was close."

Laughing, Alicia began to pour on more speed. She asked, "Are you enjoying yourself, Jeff?"

"No," Apple said wretchedly, his sore eyes scouring the way ahead on the suburban street which, at the moment, was fairly quiet. He knew that even in a normal state of sobriety he would have been terrified.

"I am having a fine time," Alicia said.

"Stop at once. Please."

"If you want me to stop, Jeff, there is a manner in which it can be done."

"What is it?"

Alicia said, "You would know it if you were with the KGB. That is what I meant by the last test."

"I only know I'm scared," Apple said. He was far too distraught and ailing to think of a way out of the predicament, and his arms weren't quite long enough to reach the handlebar controls.

"Bear gradually right," he said limply, gauging a curve in the road. "You're going too fast."

"I seem to be going too slowly," Alicia said. "I don't believe you are really frightened."

"I am, I am."

Curve taken, Alicia began to zag back and forth across the roadway. She straightened out after a horn blast sounded from behind. The driver of the car that passed shook a fist. Apple gave him a pale smile. He thought longingly of being sedated in Lilac Grange.

Alicia started to sing. She cut it off when Apple jerked out a shrill "Turn left!"

A van had pulled out of a gate. Alicia, going at a fair rip, swung away, and then, at another yell from Apple, straightened out in time from over-reacting and hitting a parked car. Apple belched.

"What's that, Jeff?"

"Bear right," he gasped.

Obeying, Alicia took them safely around the rear of the van. She asked, "Was that dangerous?"

"Too dangerous altogether."

"How wonderful."

"You have to stop."

"No, Jeff, you have to stop me."

"I don't know how," Apple said, calling it out over the engine's rising roar and the wind's batter.

"And if you jump off, you could kill yourself."

"Or be crippled for life."

"So hold on tightly," Alicia said, her voice high and gleeful. "Here we go." She shot the motor-cycle forwards.

Ahead lay a main traffic artery. Seeing it, Apple decided he couldn't take any more. It was as much the fear of throwing up as of crashing. The embarrassment would be terrible.

"There's a lame cat!" he shouted. "Stop!"

Brakes squealed and the bike swerved as it rapidly slowed. Seconds before it stopped, Apple, not trusting Alicia to stay stationary for long, stabbed both feet onto the tarmac and straightened his long legs. The motor-cycle slid from beneath him, leaving him in the middle of the roadway.

He heard another squeal of brakes, from behind. But his response was weak. Getting flattened by a truck or whatever didn't strike him as being particularly awful under the present circumstances. Ignoring the curses of a passing driver, he headed for the kerb in a turgid slump.

He arrived as Alicia finished her return from making a loop, her head back the better to see. She drew alongside with "Where's the cat?"

"I was lying," Apple said, standing as limp as string. "Sorry about that. I couldn't take any more tension."

"I see."

"I haven't been well lately. Maybe you heard Professor Warden asking about my health."

Alicia nodded. "Yes, I did," she said. Unstrapping the helmet, she took it off. "I have been thoughtless. Excuse me, please."

"Forget it, Alicia. I'm okay now. I'm simply not the hero type, that's all."

"Well, you're certainly not KGB."

"Kind of you."

Patting his shoulder, Alicia said, "Now I must give you a nice lunch, as arranged."

Apple shook his head. "Sorry. Again. I'm not up to a public scene." He knew he would never make it. Rest was what he needed. And aspirins.

"A private scene then. We can go to your London home and have a sandwich."

"Frankly, I couldn't eat a thing." While that was true,

he didn't want Alicia in Buckingham Palace with its film-baited trap. "I had a late late breakfast."

"So did I," Alicia said. "Tell you what, we will just have a cup of tea at your place."

"Ah," Apple said. He nodded slowly as though wondering if he had any cups.

"Oh dear."

"What does that mean?"

Finger to chin, Alicia asked, "You do not have a wife or something there, do you?"

"No no, of course not."

"That would be quite absurd, after all this."

"I don't have anything that even vaguely resembles a wife," Apple said. "Let's take a nice slow ride there."

After four aspirins, his head had more throb than ache and his nerves were less of a jangle, but he felt as detached from reality as *Pravda* and his eyes burned like a butler's after the house-party weekend.

All, Apple knew, from throb to burn, would be nursed into extinction by sleep. Much as he liked Alicia, he hoped she wouldn't linger after they had finished.

He asked, "Another biscuit?"

"No, thank you. I shall, however, have more tea."

Apple poured, put the pot down, reached for the sugar bowl. He held back when Alicia said, "One cube a day is enough."

"And that's how you keep your figure beautiful," Apple said, trying hard, knowing he was being a dull host.

"Thank you, Jeff. You are so nice. I am delighted that you turned out to be what you are."

"And only slipping cubes of sugar into your tea instead of poison?"

Alicia rolled her eyes melodramatically. "Or one of those truth drugs."

"Actually," Apple said, trying still, and not even thinking of the improper, "it was an aphrodisiac."

After laughing: "The things that the secret police are supposed to do are mostly fiction, I imagine."

"But you're against KGB people."

"I am against anything that is underhand. Everything ought to be above board. Or on it. Like chess."

Almost looking at his watch, Apple said, "Before we drop the subject of the KGB, for ever, how would an agent have stopped you on the bike?"

Alicia shrugged with a smile. "I have no idea. But, of course, you could have taken my helmet off."

"So I could." He looked at his watch.

"You are quite right, Jeff."

Innocently: "Mmm?"

"It is time I did the proper thing, and asked to be shown around your lovely home."

Apple managed to make the exposure of his bottom teeth look something like a smile as he got obediently up. For the sake of reality, while playing guide he made the standard deprecatory remarks about his pseudo-home. Alicia gave all the standard refusals.

She herself, after a tour of the ground floor, led the way trippingly upstairs. Her leather pants denied Apple even the bonus of seeing that upper plane of the calf.

"And what is this?" Alicia said, going into the main bedroom with a stride.

"It's a bedroom," Apple said, shuffling after.

Alicia gazed around with arms lifted, as if offering herself a pleasure. "But how very charming."

Muttering: "Thank you."

"It is so welcoming, this room, as well as being, shall we say, a little on the sensuous side."

"It's cozy."

"And do you always keep the drapes closed, Jeff, even in the daytime?"

"It runs in the family."

Alicia moved around with a hum, commenting on this and that, while Apple stood limp by the door. He looked longingly at the bed. He promised himself the sleep of his life as soon as he was able, which made him yawn. With effort, he managed to keep the sound to a squeak.

"What was that, Jeff?"

"I said I think you'll find the spare room interesting."

As though she hadn't heard, Alicia moved behind the bar, tinkered here and there, came out again and unbuttoned the top of her blouse.

She said with a seed-scattering gesture, "And this is where you bring all the young maidens."

"What?" Apple said. "Who?"

"I am not, you see, without knowledge of what goes on in the world. I am not without sophistication."

Unable to resist the call of the comfort, Apple went and sat on a corner of the bed. "No, of course not."

"There are, you know, certain signs and hints that one learns to interpret."

"I'm sure you're right."

Alicia strolled to the head of the bed. She picked up some of the reading matter, which had not been brought here from Bloomsbury, reading aloud, "*My Secret Life, Confessions of a Deaf Call Girl, Through Chelsea with Whip and Crop.*"

"Somebody left them here," Apple offered.

"Your last lady friend, naturally," Alicia said, putting the books down. She came past where Apple was sitting, trailing a hand across his shoulders as she did, and went on to the door. Gently, she pushed it closed.

Apple said a nervous "Don't touch the bolt."

"Oh, there's a bolt? Ah yes. There we are."

At the sound of the bolt being snicked home, Apple got to his feet in a struggle-won leap. He reached the threshold in four unsteady strides. He had his head down because he didn't know if all the room was now being filmed and not simply the bed area.

Stretching around Alicia, he slipped the bolt back, turned the handle, opened the door, gave a laugh like a girl being tickled, said, "That's better."

Easing away from him, her face stony, Alicia asked, "What on earth are you doing, Jeff?"

He stared at her while his weary mind battled to find an answer. He kept saying, "Look here." It was no help.

"I see," Alicia said at last. She eased even further away and her expression became haughty. "I see."

"You see what?"

"That you yourself have been doing some interpreting of signs and hints. And unfortunately you have arrived at an erroneous conclusion."

Sagging tiredly, Apple said like a broken man, "I haven't the slightest idea what you're talking about."

"That I doubt very much," Alicia said. "Everything points to the uncomfortable fact that you got completely the wrong impression about me."

"It does?"

"It does."

"What impression did I get?"

Alicia said, "You thought that I was about to act in, shall we say, a wanton manner."

Apple roused himself enough to put on a face of shock, saying a flabby "Good heavens, no. I thought no such thing, I promise you."

"Then why did you unbolt and open the door?"

"Look here."

"Precisely," Alicia said. "It is awful enough that you should get the idea that I had concupiscible designs, but that you should find the prospect unappealing . . ." She left the rest of it behind her as she stalked through the doorway.

Apple followed at a sick-man stumble, along the short hall and down the stairs. He caught up with Alicia at the front door, at which juncture he found the answer.

Talking quickly, soothingly, he explained that, as he had mentioned to her before, he had this wretched claustrophobia, as indeed she had herself, though his condition was so severe that if there was another person in a room with him he needed to have the door open.

"It's a terrible embarrassment to me. I can hardly bring myself to talk of it."

"But we had the door closed in the kitchen."

"Kitchens don't count," Apple said dismissingly.

"And at the cottage."

"As a matter of beastly fact, strangely enough, it's only bedrooms with wall-to-wall carpet and green curtains."

"Then change them."

"The landlord won't let me," Apple said.

Alicia shook her head. "Carpet and curtains?"

"You know how illogical most of these psychological conditions are. Seemingly illogical, I mean. Obviously there must be some deep-seated reason for them."

Looking less haughty, Alicia said, "Quite so. My fear of confined spaces, for instance, comes from when I got locked in a drawer as a toddler."

Intrigued despite everything, Apple asked, "What else was in the drawer besides you?"

"Lingerie."

"You're not also afraid of underwear, are you?"

"Not in the slightest."

"Anyway," Apple said, "apart from all that, our problems, I certainly reached no impressions about you, Alicia, and as for me finding you unappealing, that's downright ridiculous."

Her face and stance back to normal, Alicia said, "It was no doubt my fault, Jeff. Forget it."

"Are we still friends?"

"Certainly. More so than ever."

"Thank you."

"Now, I still owe you a meal, so how about dinner tonight?"

It was agreed that they would meet at Viscount Tower at eight o'clock, and that Alicia would now return there by taxi, since she had no legal permission to use the motorcycle. She kissed Apple and was gone. Apple headed whimperingly for bed.

FIVE

"Ahem."

Apple stirred at the sound. He was aware through his sleepy haze that he was hearing it for more than the first time. The interruption he took well. He wasn't wild about the dreams he had been having: himself in convict drag of the type that exists only in comic books, being chased by baying Rolls-Royces and howling motor-cycles.

"Ahem, ahem and ahem," the same voice said with a tinge of joking over-impatience.

Apple opened his eyes. Remembering where he was, he raised his head and looked across the Buckingham Palace master bedroom. He said, "Oh, it's you."

Leaning jauntily against the doorframe was Albert. "At last," he said. "You sleep like a lumberyard."

"I lead an active life."

"I'll say you do. With dollies like this sexy Russian chess player what surely knows a thing or two about knights." He leaned forwards on a chokey laugh.

Apple, liking Alicia, didn't care for the crack. But if he showed the latter, he could give away the former, which would work against him if it got to Angus Watkin, so he sat up with a grin. "That's neat."

Snapping to gravity like someone being hit by a dart, Albert asked, "You feel all right?"

"Like spring," Apple said. He looked at his watch. "Must get moving."

"Yes, you must. Downstairs to the kitchen. Mr. Watkin would like a word with you." He retreated.

Not even having taken off his shoes (though they hadn't soiled the spread because his feet were off the bed by several inches), Apple got up in sprightly fashion. Feeling rested and sharp, he went to the bathroom. After splashing water on his face, he went downstairs.

Angus Watkin stood with folded arms, leaning back against the sink like a plumber on overtime. "Afternoon, Porter," he said with two nods, the second directed towards the table. "Please sit down."

"Evening, sir," Apple dared as he sat. He wasn't going to let himself be totally browbeaten by this old routine, reversing the usual, of making the underling uncomfortable by having him sit while his superior stands. In any case, this showed that Watkin had very little ammunition.

"Proceed with your progress report, Porter."

In short, efficient sentences Apple told of his travails with Edward Baker. He made the complex, arduous and exhausting operation sound as simple as buying a hat.

Unexpectedly, Angus Watkin gave what amounted to praise: "Yes, that was one of several correct procedures."

"Thank you, sir."

"And it's perhaps best that you chose the simplest."

Apple sighed. "Yes."

"However," his Control said, "I'm not concerned about the side effects. What's happening with Miss Suvov?"

Blinking boyishly and keenly, Apple said, "The mission is going along splendidly, sir. The subject and I have a date this evening."

"You two have had other dates as well, Porter. They didn't take you terribly far in the desired direction."

"I'm planning a crafty campaign."

As dry as hot sand, Watkin asked, "What were you cam-

paigning craftily about earlier today when you performed
that leap off the bed upstairs?"

Apple realised that, naturally, his coming here with Alicia would have been known about, either through an
agent watching or inside the house or, more likely, by the
bolt-shooting having triggered a signal somewhere.

Wanting it known that he realised this, he said, "Ah yes,
while I slept somebody must have checked the cameras
and developed the films."

"Video tape, as a matter of fact," Angus Watkin said.
"We obtained two scintillating seconds of footage. Agent
One doing the aforementioned leap."

As though musing aloud, Apple said, "Might've been
simpler if I had been consulted before the cameras were
checked."

"It seems," Angus Watkin said heavily, "that you were
in a sleep of coma proportions, and smelling of alcohol."

"All in the line of duty, sir."

"You had been trying to get the subject drunk, Porter?"

"No, sir. The Baker business."

"Good, because, as you must be aware, films of carnal
activity in which a subject appears to have been rendered
malleable by alcohol or drugs have small value."

"Yes, sir."

"So," Watkin said, "let's get to those two seconds of ac-
tion-packed film."

"I can explain that," Apple lied airily.

"The bolt shot itself?"

"Actually, that's quite humorous, sir. The bolt sui-
cided."

Angus Watkin stared like a corpse. "I'm waiting, Porter."

"Matter of fact, funnily enough, the subject did it herself." He told himself you never knew how much Watkin
knew via the cameras or even an observer.

"I do, Porter, have a sense of humour. Pray amuse me, if you must."

Apple had it now, vaguely, more or less. He said, "I got Miss Suvov here to Buckingham Palace finally. She'd resisted hard until today. I had to pull every trick I knew. Getting her to accompany me was . . ."

"Never mind the finery, Porter," Watkin said with a twitch of his folded arms. "Just give me the frame."

"Well, after a while I induced her to go up to the bedroom. I sat on the bed and dared her to shoot the bolt. She did. I then sped to her side and slid the bolt back. This, I told her, was to show how fully I could be trusted."

Almost frowning, Angus Watkin said, "I don't know if I follow your reasoning."

"And it worked," Apple said as if deaf. "She invited me to have dinner with her tonight."

As if deafer, Watkin said, "It is not, is it, that the lady is completely unseduceable?"

Apple laughed at the very idea. "Oh no, sir. She's ready to fall anytime. After that bolt thing today, I've got her totally in my confidence."

"I suppose we'd better not go into the logic of that," Angus Watkin said. "Where's the rendezvous?"

"Viscount Tower."

"Then, of course, you will be planning to take care of any competition that might be in the field, in order to block possible interference."

"Oh, will I?"

Watkin nodded. "As soon as possible you'll make a telephone call to a police station near Viscount Tower, I know. You plan to tell them that a gang of pickpockets is working the lobby. You'll describe each man."

"Certainly," Apple said.

"The reason you're going to use this ploy is because you know it will work, since you happen to be aware of the fact that the police are used to such anonymous tips and know them to be genuine, not nuisance calls. They always come from rival gangs of pickpockets."

"That's correct, sir." He told himself that, in a manner of speaking, his future mind had been read by Angus Watkin, because he was sure to have evolved an idea as good as that sooner or later.

"I'm glad you're thinking ahead, Porter."

"Thank you, sir."

"But I mustn't keep you," Angus Watkin said. Unfolding his arms, he put a hand to his brow. "You are excused, Porter. Good evening and good trying."

Fifteen minutes later, after a shower and a change of shirt, Apple came downstairs to find the other two men gone. In the living room he made telephone calls. The first was to the car rental agency, to tell them where they could find the Ford, keys in ashtray. The second and last call was to the police at Little Venice, during which he enjoyed talking the way he imagined a pickpocket would talk while turning a rival in.

Humming, Apple went out to the motor-cycle. That he was fully recovered from his mid-day ordeal he could tell by the way he looked about as he drove, uplifted by knowing he was on stolen property. He wasn't surprised when, near Bloomsbury, as he was leaving the bike outside a police station, he was taken by a fit of loud coughing.

Briskly Apple headed for the garage where he kept Ethel.

After entering the bright, bustly lobby of Viscount Tower, Apple stopped on the threshold. He gazed around as if in that unseeing way new arrivals use while pinching their nostrils and pretending not to feel awkward.

Not one of the Seven Dwarfs was in evidence. Congratulating himself on the idea which he would have got eventually, Apple strolled to the desk. After giving a clerk the code-number of Alicia's suite, he asked him:

"Is it true what I've heard, that you had a spot of trouble here a while back?"

"Yes, sir," the clerk said, lifting a telephone receiver. He dialled along with "Several loiterers were taken away by the police for questioning."

"In connexion with what?"

"At the moment there are eleven rumoured reasons. Myself, I think the men are burglars."

"Or maybe they're just homeless."

"Quite," the clerk dead-panned. He held out the receiver. "You're through, sir."

Apple took over. "Hello. This is Jeff."

The answering voice belonged to Babushka. "Ah, the rich Mr. Poor," she said. "How are you?"

"Fine, thank you."

"And what seems to be wrong, Mr. Poor?"

A feeling of discomfort passed around Apple's waist like a hairy belt. "Nothing's wrong," he said. "I'd like to speak to Alicia, please."

"On the telephone?" Babushka asked.

"Of course."

"But how can you if she is not here?"

"Oh, I see. You mean she's still out."

Babushka said, "I mean, Mr. Poor, that she went out ten minutes ago, as you know perfectly well."

Apple straightened slowly. He asked, "As *I* know?"

The line was quiet for a moment. It came sharply alive again with "What are you talking about, please?"

"I'd like to ask you that same question."

Babushka said, "Is Alicia not with you?"

Apple straightened still more. He said, "No, she isn't."

From the agitated boom that followed, Apple gathered unhappily that Jeff Poor had telephoned ten minutes ago to say that plans were changed and would Alicia meet him elsewhere. She had agreed and gone.

Apple looked all around the lobby as if for an answer, if not the sight of Alicia. Gaining nothing, he said into the receiver, "Where did she go? Which elsewhere?"

Babushka asked a harsh "You did not telephone?"

"No, I didn't. I know nothing about it. I last saw Alicia several hours ago."

From the other end came a splurge of Russian. Apple stemmed it with "Wait. Hold on. Let's not get excited."

"Why not?"

"Because there's sure to be some very simple solution to this." He didn't believe that but he didn't want to start a panic going. "Now listen. Did Alicia say where she was going to meet me?"

"No, she did not. No names."

"Oh great."

"Only that it was the usual spot."

"Right," Apple snapped in an action-stations voice. "Hold everything. I'll go and check." He slapped down the receiver and turned.

Making his way without attention-drawing haste across the lobby, Apple told himself that this could well be another of Alicia's tests, and perhaps Babushka was in on it. He wasn't too convincing.

As he passed outside onto the forecourt, a man stepped into his path. "Excuse me."

Apple brushed by firmly, saying, "Sorry, I never buy lottery tickets."

Next he was off the forecourt and striding along the lamplit street. His aim was the square where he had met Alicia and returned her, which, he reasoned, could be the only place she had meant.

After turning the first corner, Apple began to run. That

he was staying reasonably calm over this strangeness was because he couldn't believe that it meant anything too desperate. He also thought it might be connected to that stupid pickpocket idea of Watkin's.

Apple soon arrived at the square, which had bright lighting. He went around it, still running. There was no sign of Alicia. Again he ran a circuit, this time on the inner pavement, beside the parklet railings. There was no sign of Alicia. He stood near the area where he had met her and looked in all directions. There was no sign of Alicia. Entering the parklet, he peered behind every bush and tree. There was no sign of Alicia.

Out again on a corner, he cupped his hands to his mouth and shouted her name. A dog barked, a curtain parted for a peeker, a couple changed from stroll to march and Apple felt a minor blush heat his temples, but—there was no sign of Alicia.

With considerably less calm, Apple started back for Viscount Tower. He walked, the better to think, until he found he had nothing to think about, no possibilities to juggle with; then he began to run. He slowed only on turning the last corner so that his fluster wouldn't be seen.

When he was almost at the forecourt, a man approached. He, Apple saw, was the same one as a few minutes ago and not one of the Dwarfs. He had thinning hair, a tough-ugly face, a suit that screamed its cheapness and a tie that simpered its luxury price-tag.

As the man, one speechmaker hand raised, was opening his mouth to start, Apple said, "Excuse me." He quickened his pace to cover the remaining yards.

The moment Apple went into Viscount Tower, he saw he had another problem, one of a different nature. Babushka was there, by the desk, talking to a tall man in a sober suit; a man who had "cop" stamped on his every facet.

Apple started to curve into a turn, on his way to making an exit. But he was too late. Babushka saw him. With the tall man in pursuit, she came bulling across the lobby. Her face was as set as a wooden mask. Apple went forwards.

They met half-way. Babushka burst out in a subdued, public-place manner, "She was not there, was she? I knew she would not be."

Apple said, "Take it easy."

The man loomed close. His frown seemed deeper because of the fact that he had to aim it upwards. He asked, "Your name is Jeff Poor?"

"That's right. Who're you?"

"Swinton. I'm head of security here."

Relieved not to be dealing with a policeman and determined to keep it that way, Apple said soothingly to them both, "Everything's going to be all right."

"Is it?" Swinton asked. "We'll see about that." He looked as though this was his first case in years and he wasn't going to let it go until they were parted by death. "This is all most peculiar."

"What is?"

"I'll ask the questions, Poor. And we'll start with this one. Did you telephone Miss Alicia Suvov a while ago and ask her to meet you somewhere?"

Babushka said, "No, he didn't."

Apple said, "Yes, I did."

Everyone exchanged unsmiling glances, as though playing a guessing game for money. Babushka looked bewildered; she, Apple thought, appeared to be genuinely worried. The security man looked deeply inflamed; he, Apple realised, had probably just had his wings clipped in connexion with the apprehension of alleged pickpockets on his territory.

Babushka accused Apple, "You told me that you did not telephone Alicia."

Swinton said, "The receptionist just told me he doesn't recall much about the man who made that first call, but he certainly wasn't a giant."

This was getting messier and trickier, Apple mused while furiously trying to find an out. He said, "I shall ignore the insult to my person."

"That's the way, Poor."

"I'll simply mention that the man who called wasn't just any old body."

The others both asked, "Who was he?"

Apple had it. He said, "The Secretary of the Alicia Suvov Fan Club."

Babushka: "The Secretary is a woman."

"I meant her father."

"Her father has been dead for years."

Noting the rapidly growing suspicion in Swinton's eyes, Apple decided that that angle wasn't it after all. He said with a shy smile, "All right, I give in. I can see I'll have to tell you the truth."

Babushka nodded and the security man took in a long breath through his nose. Apple said, "I just hope Alicia understands, that's all."

Swinton asked, "What does that mean?"

"It means that I did try. But you got the truth out of me, both of you. It doesn't follow that I'm jealous or anything like that. Certainly not."

Swinton: "I wish I knew what you were talking about."

Apple stopped wishing similar. To Babushka he said, "You remember Edward Baker, I know."

"Of course I do."

"Well, that first call was from him. He had arrived in England not long before. His plane was delayed." Voice getting drabber and mien gloomier, Apple went on to tell about the ground-staff strike in New York, filling time with the defusingly mundane. His audience obliged, eas-

ing off on the tip-toe tension. The suspicion in Swinton's
eyes became a suspicion of an innocent explanation.

"When he telephoned Alicia and asked her to meet him
at once," Apple said to Babushka, "she told you it was me
calling."

"Why did she do that, Mr. Poor?"

"Because she feels that you don't approve of Edward
Baker, she said. I saw her just now, by accident, with him.
They've gone for dinner."

Babushka, face normal, was nodding slowly. The security man looked at her sidelong with heavy-eyed disappointment.

Apple said, "Alicia sent me back here to calm your worries. She asked me to tell you some lie or another. Oh
well." He shrugged. "I did try."

"It is perfectly all right," Babushka said. "I will mention nothing of this. I am sorry about Mr. Baker. I hope
you do not feel too hurt."

Holding on, Swinton said an unconvincing "I don't really understand what's going on here."

"The young lady will explain," Apple said forlornly.
He would have hung his head save for knowing that, at his
height, it never had the right effect. "I have another er-
rand to run."

Swinton: "Good night."

"Giants never win."

Babushka began, "Well—"

"No no," Apple said softly, holding out a staying hand.
"Please don't say anything." Distantly, he wondered if he
was being a mite heavy with the acting. "Fate has decided." He brought the hand back to form a clasp with the
other. "Time will take care of it all."

"I imagine it will."

"Farewell for now."

"Good-bye, Mr. Poor."

Anxiously: "Please call me Jeff."

Babushka closed one eye thoughtfully. "Thank you."

Apple bowed, turned, moved off. When he glanced behind a moment later on his way out, the security man was drably chewing his thumb nail and Babushka still had that one eye closed in doubt.

First, he thought, try back at the square. Second, telephone to Buckingham Palace to see if that was the place she meant. Third, have a discreet word with the reception clerk who had seen the first caller.

"Hang on, mate."

Apple, crossing the forecourt, saw that he was being addressed by the same man as before, who was turning up the collar of his cheap suit against a sprinkle of rain.

"Sorry," Apple said, passing. "No tickets left."

"Don't know what you mean," the man said. "This is about Alice Suvov."

Stopping fast, turning slowly, Apple asked, "What is?"

"Me, mate," the man said. He stood average height, and on closer examination his face was more ugly than tough. "And you."

For something to say Apple corrected, "It's Alicia, by the by, not Alice."

"What's in a name, as the Bard complained. It's what the dolly fetches that matters."

"Do you speak Greek as well as Double Dutch? If so, do you come bearing gifts?"

"This ain't getting us anywhere," the man said, his manner a shade nervous. "Maybe you're the wrong geezer." He wiped rainwater off his thinning hair.

"Maybe I am," Apple said, growing more interested because he sensed that he had found the answer. "Try me and see."

"We're looking for a go-between, see. You know Alice, so we thought you'd fit the bill nicely."

"Going between who or what?"

"Us and Alice's lot—her family or even the whole Commie government. It don't make no difference to us. Except we don't want foreign lolly."

With rain pattering on his head, Apple stated, "You know where she is, of course."

"Right," the man said with a wary glance around, like a deer at the pool. He was tense but unafraid. "By the by, mate, if you was thinking of trying anything off your own bat, in the old violence department like—forget it. I could break you in two dead easy."

"Never mind that. Let's get the facts out. I want to know where Alicia is."

"Somewhere safe. And she'll stay that way, safe and unhurt, till we get our money. Which should be quick. If this thing drags on, we can't be responsible for Alice's comfort or health or anything else. So let's get on the ball, lofty. I'm sure you don't want to see the young lady come to harm."

During this speech Apple had recognised the criminal pattern. In the past year, sub-celebrity snatching had been popular. The kidnapped victims were never too famous, never from wealthy or powerful families, never connected in any way with politics, never male. Always, the kidnapping only came to public light when it was all over, within hours, the victim freed for a sum of money that wasn't so excessive as to be unraisable, which would mean bringing in the police. At no point was the hostage threatened with death; only minor violence and sexual abuse.

"Alicia makes the perfect victim," Apple allowed, glad at least that the mystery was solved.

"We been trying to cop her for days," the man said as if in agreement. "But look, mate, I'm getting wet."

"You're not the only one, mate."

"Right. So then, let me ask you, are you on as the go-between in this lark?"

Apple said, "I would be, yes, if I were sure you had Alicia and that she's unharmed."

Like a peace marcher, the man shuffled aggressively. "What you mean? Ain't you been listening?"

"Acutely. But before I accept the part, I want to speak to Alicia and be convinced. The best thing you can do is take me to where you've got her hidden."

"Don't be effing stupid, mate."

"Then suppose I simply report this to the police?"

"In that case, what we do is, we enjoy ourselves with the lady and then let her go. Better luck next time, that's how we look at it."

Not caring for the understatement of "enjoy," Apple said, "The telephone then. If I can speak to Miss Suvov on the blower, I'll be satisfied."

"That, yes," the man said. "That we can do. You'll be in touch anyway till this is over, you and Sammy."

"Sammy's the boss?"

"No bosses, mate, just sections of activity. But let's get to a blower. Follow me."

Rather than follow, Apple preferred to stay close beside. As they walked along through the light rain, he said, "Might be convenient if I had a name for you."

"Joseph. I've always fancied that one. Joseph."

"Well, Joseph, did you lot pull that snatch on the Welsh actress last summer?"

"Ask me no questions and I'll tell you no lies," the man said. "Yes."

"Neat," Apple said.

Lolling slightly, Joseph said, "Yeah."

"But what stumps me is how you got Alicia to come out.

Or rather, how you were able to imitate my voice. You or Sammy."

"Your voice? No, there was no imitating, as you'll learn when you read all about it in the popular press. Alice was called by a voice she didn't know."

"Somehow, I thought it would be like that," Apple said, feeling he was taking the right casual line. "Clever."

"The lady was simply told that someone was in trouble. No names. But she could guess. This was urgent. She'd best get there quick and keep mum about it. See, it's what you *don't* say that counts."

It raised Apple's chin that Alicia had responded so quickly and willingly when she thought he needed help. Now, he thought, it was his turn.

Joseph looked up. "See, it's what they call psychological something or another."

"Brilliant," Apple said, whereupon he realised the why of his "neat" and "clever" and "brilliant." If these people were put up to an okay level, above the mere brutish, he could more readily accept his own hostage arrangements.

Feeling prickly about that, he huffed, "But wrong, criminal, disgraceful."

Joseph said, "Balls."

Which was the last verbal exchange between them until they came to a street telephone booth. They squeezed in together. The door closed but Apple, out of habit, pushed it partway open again with his foot.

Joseph asked, "What d'you think you're playing at, mate?" After listening to Apple explain about his claustrophobia, he said, "We either have the door closed or we don't make no telephone calls."

Reminding himself that this was for Alicia, Apple drew the door closed and clenched his knee-caps. "Let's go."

Joseph lifted the receiver, fed the coin slot. He named

the numerals as he dialled them, after saying, "Remember this. It's the number you'll be using."

When the line clicked to life, he said, "It's me. I got the tallish fella. He wants to talk to our Alice. Okay?" He handed the receiver to Apple, who heard a thud of footsteps, which, since there was no fade in or out, meant that the telephone was being carried.

The footsteps stopped and he heard "Hello. This is Alicia Suvov speaking."

"Jeff here."

Her tone throbbed relief. "Oh, it's you. Thank heavens. The voice of sanity among all this mad awfulness."

"How are you?"

"I'm fine. I think. But I'm frightened. What—"

The line cut off. Taking back the receiver and dropping it in its cradle, Joseph said, "There you are, mate. Do we have her or don't we?"

"I'm convinced," Apple said. He pushed out into the rain. "How much d'you want?"

Joseph followed. "First we need to know if her people're going to play. Meaning pay up nice and fast—and quiet. So you find that out and give us a ring."

"I don't think there's going to be a lot of money involved," Apple said while his eyes were flitting rapidly, covering the street, weighing possibilities.

"Our Alice, she must earn bloody thousands in all them chess games she wins."

"The chess world isn't quite like that," Apple murmured absently. The street was fairly busy, he noted, with many pedestrians and vehicles, plus nearby a long queue of commuters stretching along the kerb from a bus-stop. The sole drawback was the brightness: stark blue-toned lamps above, lights of traffic below.

"Look, I can't stand here all night," Joseph said. "This rain's ruining my suit."

"It's not doing mine the world of good, either."

"Get going, mate. That way. Don't look back. And don't waste any time about calling us."

If he was so concerned about his crappy suit, surely he wouldn't stand in the rain until the go-between had finally faded from sight. He would assume him to continue being the nice, tame person he had presented himself to be, one who wouldn't dream of throwing a look behind.

Thus the reasoning of Apple as he went along the street. He slowed his pace, at the same time sagging slightly at the knees, which sag he allowed to increase, knowing that to an observer the shrinkage in height could seem to be due to distance, perspective.

After another dozen slow paces, finding himself among a scrum of pedestrians, and having by now reduced himself to average height, Apple made an abrupt side turn and stepped into the gutter.

He rounded a parked car to the roadway. There, crouching, he started to go back towards the telephone booth. Even if his change of course had been seen by Joseph, he mused, it couldn't make matters any the worse.

Stopping, Apple cautiously raised his head above the parked vehicles. He glimpsed the other man just as he swung around to leave, striding past the telephone booth and going behind the queue of people.

Apple went on. He stayed in the road. When the line of stationary cars ended, where the space reserved for buses began, he moved into the gutter. In a low crouch, like someone trying to pull up his socks while still in motion, he went along in front of the bus queue.

The waiting people, most of them under umbrellas, gazed down at him Britishly; that is, with stolid interest but prepared to deny on the instant that they were even looking in that direction.

Apple stumped on. He held his head up at a supercilious angle from the folded body, as though he were doing the people a favour by being there.

The queue ended, parked cars began. Seeing Joseph ahead in the near distance, moving away, Apple increased his height by several degrees and put on speed. He declined to recall that for a moment back there he had been tempted to shock the people by doing something bizarre, which declining was out of shame at not having had the nerve to do it.

With his head bobbing at about car-roof level, Apple stayed in the roadway. Traffic being slow, the only dangers came from Joseph making a flash turn and seeing him, and from him catching pneumonia.

Apple told himself that he could always get an umbrella, of course. Apart from using it in the obvious way, what you did was burn a hole in it with a cigarette (all done without even breaking step) and peep your way along in hidden pursuit.

When buying an umbrella was out, shops being closed or appropriate one not available, you helped yourself to what was around. You unhooked from passing elbow, took down from peg in private hallway, lifted from brollystand in public establishment, snatched from hand of child.

In the spy game, Apple mused defensively, the end justified the meanies. And you could always drop the Chamberlain off at a lost-property office.

But there was the risk of being caught in the act, Apple thought. With a smile of horror he pictured himself trying to rip free from the grab of a wailing brat that wanted its dumb umbrella back.

Apple was pleased to note, as the man ahead turned into a quiet street, that the rain had slackened off.

Joseph stopped beside a pick-up truck. Its cab was hidden by the wall of large cartons that came midway along the bed to the tailgate.

Joseph looked around in the cursory fashion of confidence. He skimmed straight over the car behind which Apple stooped, opened the driver's door of the truck and got in. The engine growled to life, the lights came on, the outside indicator started to blink.

As the truck edged out of its parking slot, Apple, who was still on the same side of the street, went over the kerb and ran lightly along the pavement. He was out of view of Joseph's side-mirrors.

A car went by. When it had passed, the truck drove out. At the same time, Apple reached the tailgate. With the greatest of ease, he vaulted over it onto the truck bed. Nothing to it, he thought.

Sitting, he got himself into a central position. He was still congratulating himself on his success when the truck lunged to a higher speed—and started to buck. Its springs were like concrete.

Apple bounced. With contact shared by his flat hands and his buttocks and his heels, he bounced rhythmically on the rain-sodden wood. Squeaks and clatter kept in time.

Head unavoidably nodding as if at the beat, jaw clenched against chatter, Apple continued bouncing. He went back and forth and from side to side on the truck floor like a pea on a kettledrum. Not only was he uncomfortable, the seat of his pants grew soaking wet.

Nor was relief due in the form of the truck slowing or being held up by traffic lights, Apple realised: Joseph had gone onto a thruway.

Since standing might be dangerous, to his person and the secrecy of his presence, Apple tried a squat. At once he fell over. He bounced on his back. Up again he tried all-fours. The wood hurt his knees. He returned to a sit.

Not caring for his suspicion that the situation was not

so much harrowing as farcical, Apple tried to ignore his non-stop bouncing. He couldn't find anything else to think about. He started whistling, but stopped when his tune took on the beat of the bounce.

A double-decker bus had been slowly catching up. Now it drew out in order to pass. However, noticing Apple, the driver steered back into the inside lane again and came close. He watched solemnly.

Not so the trio of acne-clad youths on the front seat above. Of a sudden they switched from gapes to hilarity. They pointed, they fell about, they doubled over, they punched one another. Faintly their yells could be heard, like the cries of distant seagulls.

Apple pretended to be unaware of his audience. Having discovered by now that he could manoeuvre to some degree by plying his hands and heels, he started to turn himself in a bouncy circle, the while staring vacantly straight ahead like an old photograph.

For a while his back was turned to the bus. The circle, however, curled on. Soon he came around to face front again. The driver was still solemn. In the window above, half a dozen other passengers had come forwards, were grinning from behind the weepy, helpless youths.

Apple closed his eyes.

He didn't snap them open until he felt himself lurching from a swerve. The bus had gone and so had the thruway, he saw. The truck he was on, its speed reduced, was moving along a quiet residential street with dim lighting. The bouncing had stopped.

They turned into another street. It was even dimmer than the first on account of its huge trees. After the grind of gears being changed, the truck slowed still more and the nearside direction signal began to flash red.

Apple quickly crawled to the back, where he slipped over the tailgate.

Recalling from Training Five that you should always get off a moving vehicle by facing in the same direction, Apple easily managed to maintain his footing. Head down, he darted into the side of the road and got behind a tree's fat trunk. He peered out.

A short distance ahead, Joseph was steering through a gateway. There was no gate and the brick posts were in an advanced state of decay. Up from one of them poked a notice-board, not itself in the freshness of youth. It said that this desirable six-bed property was for sale.

All was silence when the truck's engine and lights were switched off. Next came the sound of its door being slammed, a clap of shoes on paving stones, and last the thud of a house door.

Apple stepped out from behind his tree. He went to the crumbly gate. From there it was a gentle downslope to the house, which stood bulky and dark and shuttered. It was also ugly, one of those semi-Gothic loomers built on the minimum of ground by Edwardian speculators. Even though the neighbouring houses showed light, they were equally as gloomy.

Going down the slope, Apple passed the truck and went quietly to the nearest window. Its shutters were firm and he could hear nothing from beyond. It was the same at every window he tried on the lower level as he began a circle around the building.

Light gleamed faintly from under the kitchen door, but cautious pressure on the wood proved that bolts were at home at both top and bottom. Apple moved on.

He had no plan in mind, other than to try to make an entry. What he would do then he didn't know. About his safety he had minor concern, since he reckoned that the kidnappers would resort to only the non-lethal forms of violence. Apple knew that what he reckoned and what

was true were often worlds apart, but he frequently ignored what he knew in favour of what he would like to
know.

Just before reaching the house entrance, on his full circuit, Apple saw a drainpipe. Rather, he saw that the pipe
passed near a possible point of access on the upper floor.
Unshuttered French windows stood behind a railing, a
skimpy balcony of the type that exist more for decor than
utility.

Grasping the pipe, Apple tested for movement, play on
the wall-fastenings. There was none. Furthermore, the
pipe itself had the solidity of its era. The recent rain, however, had rendered the metal slippery.

Pros and cons weighed, Apple decided to chance it. He
began to go up, climbing in approved fashion: hands as
though they were on a rope, feet as if they were walking.
As long as he kept pressure on his feet, he knew, it was
impossible to fall. He looked neither up nor down.

When he had ascended some two metres from the
ground, he heard a scraping. Quickly he looked up. The
fastening was coming away from the wall. So was the
pipe.

Apple held still, watching. The length of pipe continued to come out towards him until, with a final sound not
unlike a death rattle, the fastening came free, and fell.

It was only a split second after he had raised his hands
to protect himself, deflect the falling chunk of metal, that
Apple realised he had let go of his hold. He started to fall.
In doing so he made a wild, one-handed, straw-clutching
grab for the pipe. His grip held. He brought the pipe
down with him.

They landed together side by side—Apple well and silently, the eight-foot length of piping with a boom like a
horn in the Alps. The noise seemed shatteringly loud in
the quiet street.

Waving his hands shushingly, even though aware that it would do no good, Apple backed off. When, from inside the house, he heard a thud, he swung around and raced into the bushes of the jungly front garden. He dropped flat. The flora was sodden.

From inside the building sounded more thuds. Next, with a creaking, the broad front door drew slowly inwards. At a hesitant pace a man came out onto the step, upper body in an outward lean and arms on the dangle. He looked around with a sneer of suspicion.

Tall, broad in the shoulders, age in the thirties, wearing jeans and a seaman's jersey, the man had Eurasian features and matching straight black hair. He looked the type who would rather fight a gorilla than beat up a weakling.

A voice from inside the house, faint but recognisable as belonging to Joseph, asked, "Anything up?"

The man turned his head aside to answer. "I don't see nothing wrong." His accent bore the stamp "Made in Liverpool."

"Of course you don't. Why should you? I don't know what you're so jittery about."

"Jittery? Who's bloody jittery?"

Joseph said, "Forget it."

"Nothing to be jittery about," the Eurasian said, standing straighter and losing his sneer.

"You're right."

"You and me, we could stand off an army here."

"Won't come to that, Sammy. Relax."

The man turned to go back in the house. "Yeah," he said. "But when's that long-legged idiot going to call?" He closed the door behind him.

When all sound from inside had faded, Apple got damply up. He went to the house. With a pale smile of guilt he picked up the length of pipe. After lying it neatly alongside the wall, he went to the front door.

He peered close in the dimness. As he had thought from not having heard any clicks of mechanism, the door was unlocked. A padlock and chain of giant size hung from a sprocket. Sammy and Joseph, obviously, were treating themselves to illicit use of the house.

Apple pressed against the door. It gave, but at once, even with the gap at merely an inch, its hinges began to creak. Apple had the answer to this situation, however.

Positioning himself correctly, facing the wood and as close to it as he could get, he took a right-hand clasp on the door and shot it inwards with a fast straightening of his arm. There were no creaks.

Easing himself through the space, he came into a room-size vestibule. Its flooring of traditional black and white tiles had a litter of dust and yellowing junk mail. In the inner wall's middle were frosted glass double doors of the swing variety. Apple went there on tip-toe and squinted with one eye through the separating slit.

It was a baronial hall, the floor several steps down from the swing doors. A gallery ran around above. Lighting came from the score of candles in bottles on a centre table, which was the only piece of furniture apart from a high-back chair. The chair stood at the hall's rear. In it sat Alicia. Her wrists were tied to the chair arms.

On the left was a fireplace, by which lounged Sammy, an elbow on the mantel, while Joseph, at the table, was lighting a cigarette from one of the candles.

Wait a minute, Apple thought at the end of slow nods, I've seen this movie before.

It was obvious now. This had as much relation to reality as a blue plastic duck. That wouldn't matter so much if it weren't for the fact that Alicia was terrified. Nobody seemed to have thought of that aspect of the business. But then, this was part of the spy game.

The kidnapping, Apple mused on, had to be the work of Angus Watkin. Seeing the seduction caper as failing, he had decided that it needed a little help. It was a decision he would have made gladly, for such operations within operations were his chicken and wine.

In addition to them suiting him personally, feeding his love of the convoluted, these capers enabled him to give idle hands work to do, as well as forming an important training ground for neophyte agents. They were all-round good, in fact, except for the innocent people who might be hurt or inconvenienced, but that had never deterred Angus Watkin for one thin moment.

Apple would have thought further in this vein, enjoyed a thorough vilification of his Control, if it hadn't been that he remembered Edward Baker, the innocent prisoner. With a soundless clearing of his throat Apple hurried his thoughts back to the present situation's obviousness.

First, it was unlikely that real snatchers would have chosen Jeff Poor as their go-between. Next, there was the ease with which he had been able to tail Joseph, to mention nothing of the marvellous convenience of an open-back truck to ride on. Then, at the decaying old house beloved of screen creepies, Sammy, in response to a noise, had come out slowly enough to allow the snooper to hide, and then had gratuitously given away that there were only two villains to be dealt with inside. Finally, there was the pure theatricality of this setting, with melodrama sniggering in every corner.

The point of it all, Apple knew, was the creation of gratitude. Angus Watkin expected Alicia to respond favourably, meaning be liberal with her favours, after she had been rescued from peril by her dashing new friend.

Apple, still peeking between the swing doors, sighed. He thought he was sighing because he would never be able to tell Angus Watkin that his sense of theatre was absurdly exaggerated, too corny for words; actually, Apple's sigh was for the sad fact that this scene wasn't true.

The swing doors flew open with a crash.

Apple, grim of face, landed well from his burst-through leap: feet spread, body in a slight crouch, arms out. It was the way a Robin Hood would look after springing down from a tree, Apple hoped, and not a pose that could be seen as in any way resembling the stance of unarmed combat.

Since neither Appleton Porter, philologist, nor Jeff Poor, newspaper reporter, would know anything about such sophisticated fighting methods, they had to be avoided for Alicia's sake if she was to be kept in the dark.

At the moment, however, Alicia looked as though she would not have noticed if the newcomer had been wearing purple tights. *He was here, he was sanity, she was no longer alone*, her eyes said as she sagged forwards from the chair's high back.

With the crash of the doors still echoing around the hall, Sammy stood bolt upright on the hearth and Joseph slowly moved out from the table. Both, now that Apple knew the score, seemed caricatures, especially Sammy, who could have stepped right out of Fu Manchu.

With the last echo gone, everyone became vocal at roughly the same time. Apple shouted, "Nobody move!" Alicia called out his name. Sammy snarled a what-the-hell. Joseph said, "I'll get him." Which made the Eurasian turn his snarl that way with "Well, you brought him, you bloody lunatic." Joseph denied this in dubious bluster, Apple told Alicia not to worry, everything was going to be just fine, and she told him to be careful, these men were awful thugs, gangsters, animals.

"Quiet!" Sammy roared. Having come out from the fireplace, he was on the opposite side of the central table from Joseph. "Everybody be quiet!"

Into the resulting silence Apple said an authoritative "The place is surrounded."

"Sure it is," Joseph said, breathing like the loser in a footrace. "You got tanks and all kindsa stuff out there."

"No, but we've got dozens of policemen."

"And we have to walk out as nice as can be with our little hands on our heads."

"You've guessed it."

Joseph said, "Joke over, mate. You're alone, and you're in trouble. You've annoyed me. I don't like being annoyed."

Tersely, Sammy told him, "Get him away from the door. We'll put him to night-night and then find another go-between. *I'll* find another go-between."

"Just wait," Alicia said. "You scoundrels are going to fall afoul of the law."

"Well, shit a brick," Joseph threw away as he began to arc towards Apple, who told him to watch his mouth but somehow managed not to call him a knave.

Sammy ordered, "Don't waste too much time with long-cods. Do him sharpish."

Joseph, who was now about two metres from Apple, and in a similar crouch, as if the seat of his pants were equally as wet, made a sudden flick with his hand.

The lit cigarette flew sparkily past Apple's head. Nice bit of theatre, Apple thought as he straightened like a regular guy and took on the stance of something vaguely like a John L. Sullivan.

Joseph came rushing forwards like a bull. Evidently he was also intent on not giving away a spook background, while letting himself be routed by the hero of the scene.

Apple stepped aside. Joseph went past. Snorting, he halted and turned. As he did, Apple took one stride forwards and threw up a kick. It was the kick of an amateur, that of a footballer when he misses. And Apple missed.

Nine intended victims out of ten would have ended the matter right there by grabbing the upflung foot. Joseph ignored it. Rushing in, he grappled with Apple, thereby saving him from falling backwards.

Balance recovered, Apple realised that, despite the corn, he wanted to look good in front of Alicia. The schoolboyishness of that irked him so much that he flung his opponent off with real force.

Joseph careened in arm-waving reverse to the wall, which he hit with a thump. There was a fractional pause before his face sprang on an expression of shock and pain. Gasping, "Oh, me disc," he started to slide down the wall like spilt honey.

Fast thinking, Apple allowed, as he turned the other way to see what the rest of the opposition was up to.

Sammy was coming. In one hand he held a cosh, a short length of lead pipe, which he waved back and forth in front of him as though he were spraying water. His baddy grin was beautifully done.

Alicia called to Apple to be careful. Joseph, sitting with outspread legs, his back to the wall, was still whimpering about his damaged disc.

Abruptly Sammy took a great leap forwards. At the same time, he swung his weapon up like an underhand punch. The move was impressive, even though he missed by at least a foot.

Apple backed away, still in a John L. pose. He said things like *You won't get away with this*, as well as other recalled lines of standard dialogue, while Sammy, following, did fairly well with snarls and threats. Joseph and Alicia had fallen silent, watching.

Sammy leapt in again. Unfortunately, Apple made his

own forward leap at the same moment, having grown to dislike the act of backing away.

They collided with ugly thuds. Apple's chin crashed against the top of the Eurasian's head. He went weak and dizzy and his legs felt like lettuce. With a fast embrace he held on. Sammy was doing the same, though not so much holding on as up, keeping Apple erect. They shuffled around with all the spirit of marathon dancers. Drearily, Apple was sure he must look ridiculous.

Which, when he had recovered, made him conclude that enough was enough. After all, the whole thing was an insult to his intelligence, as well as no picnic for Alicia.

Under the sound-cover of their gasps and growls, Apple said, "This is you out, mate." He brought up his knee. Although it landed innocuously on the upper thigh, the blow had force and Sammy reacted as though a bull's eye had been scored.

With a stifled, retching groan, he dropped the lead pipe and made a two-handed grab for his crotch. He doubled down to the floor like a Buddhist at prayer.

Unaware that his walk had a faint swagger, Apple strode to the back of the hall. At the chair he stooped to put comforting hands on Alicia. "Everything's okay now," he said. "It's smiling time."

"But hurry," she gasped, unsmiling. "Look."

Glancing behind as he straightened, Apple saw that although Sammy was still folded down groaningly, Joseph had started to push himself up the wall and was wearing his mouth in a twist of determination.

Built-in suspense, Apple thought sourly.

"Untie me quickly," Alicia said.

Not entirely a willing stooge, and with his chin still aching from that collision with the Eurasian's head, Apple took his fumbled time about freeing the first wrist from its length of frayed rope. Sensing again Alicia's fear, however, he hurried with the second binding.

Sammy, giving up on groans, raised his head, while Joseph, fully erect against the wall, seemed to be wondering what he should do with his manifested belligerence.

Released, Alicia jumped to her feet as though ejected from the chair. She semi-fell against Apple with a gasped "Let us run, Jeff."

He took her by the hand and pulled her along behind him as he loped towards the swing doors. To Sammy, sitting up, he gave a wide berth, not caring for any more nonsense.

Joseph, as they neared, made a lunge out from the wall. But he seemed as lost as an actor stricken with sudden amnesia. He merely flapped his arms like a kindergarten teacher at a playground fight.

Apple towed Alicia past, up the steps, through the swing doors, across the vestibule and outside. He would have been satisfied to stop there, but Alicia went by him to become the tower. She led him at a run onto and along the street, which pattered with a return of the drizzle.

The past incident Apple saw as outright silly, in respect of both implementation and conception. Did Angus Watkin, he thought, really expect the subject to fling herself into Agent One's arms with gladsome cries of "My hero!"?

At the street end they stopped under a tree, panting. They smiled at one another. Alicia put a hand on Apple's shoulder. She squeezed and said, "My hero."

SIX

Apple was furious. Had he been alone, he would have kicked the tree trunk or thudded fist into palm. That Angus Watkin was right he found intolerable. It was like an I-told-you-so situation wherein the other person didn't remember being told so. Apple let his smile waste away.

And now as Alicia swayed towards him, her face raised and her lips seeming to offer an invitation, he said unbendingly, cool as a queue-jumper:

"Hero? Not at all, not at all."

"Oh, but yes."

"It was nothing. Any man would have done the same under those circumstances."

Alicia eased back. "No, Jeff. It was very brave of you, heroic, tackling two criminals like that."

"Bravery, they say, is nine-tenths stupidity."

"Please. I will not have you decry your achievement, your selflessness. They could have killed you."

"They didn't seem the type for murder."

Alicia shook her head the way little girls do at naughty dolls. "Anyway, I thank you very much for rescuing me."

Less cool, Apple said, "It was my pleasure. Really."

After patting his shoulder, Alicia brought down her hand and looked at it. "You are wet."

"A bit. I'll tell you about that later. First, as soon as possible, we have to let your friend Irini know that everything's all right."

"How did she know I was in trouble? Did these criminals make contact already? And how did you enter the scene? Oh, I have a hundred questions."

"I'll tell you everything that happened," Apple said, "while we're finding a telephone. Come on."

"We ought not to stay around here in any case," Alicia said with a worried glance behind. "Let us hurry."

As they went at a brisk pace through the lamplit, drizzly streets, Apple lost the remainder of his annoyance and declined firmly to dwell on the subject of unfair influence. With Alicia's hand warm in his own, he told of his toil, starting at the opening talk with Babushka on the Viscount Tower house telephone, including the meeting with her and the security man and then Joseph, and ending at his burst-in appearance at the Karloffesque house. Of bouncing around on trucks he made no mention.

Coming to a public telephone booth, they went in together. It was a tight squeeze, Apple was glad to note, after he had thrust an arm back to keep him away from the side, and not once did he think of his claustrophobia, except to wonder in passing why he wasn't feeling claustrophobic.

When she was connected with Babushka, Alicia rattled in her own language. She told what had transpired from the time, in the square, that she had been bundled into a car by two men. From the other end came a series of shocked squeaks, like insulted mice.

When it was Babushka's turn to rattle, it was Alicia's turn to be shocked, though once she giggled. There was no reply to Apple's repeated "What is it?" He had to content himself with the give and take of body pressure, the while ignoring his wet bottom.

Alicia put the receiver down. She said, "No one there knows of the kidnapping. But Irini guessed from your odd behaviour that something was amiss."

"I knew she wasn't completely fooled."

"But why did you try to hide the situation, rather than raise the alarm?"

Truthfully, Apple said, "I thought it was another of your tests or something like that."

Nodding, Alicia said, "But guess what. Viscount Tower is crawling with newspaper reporters, all looking for me."

"How come?"

"And you."

Apple straightened. "Looking for me?"

"Looking for us both, Jeff," Alicia said. "There is a rumour, it appears, that you and I are engaged."

"Engaged? Matrimony and all that?"

"A betrothal, yes."

Apple began to nod slowly. This, he realised, just had to be the revenge of the Dwarfs, who, of course, would soon have come to the conclusion that the tall interloper was responsible for them being taken in for questioning.

Playing the innocent philologist, however, he asked, "Where did the press get that idea from?"

"Reporters are strange people, especially in the spring of the year."

"I still don't see what's so newsworthy about you getting engaged to someone unfamous like me."

"A Red and a White getting together is good human-interest material," Alicia said, patting his chest. "Furthermore, did you know that sometimes the tabloids refer to me as Icy Alice?"

"Bloody cheek," Apple said with a fairly good show of blinking outrage. It was only natural, he assured himself, that he would slide a protective arm around Alicia's shoulders.

The curious way her height now increased was due, he realised after the first surprise, to the fact that she had risen on her toes. Their faces were reasonably close. They became more so as Apple started to lower his head, lean down towards the waiting lips.

The noise crashed around the confined space like sharp words in a vestry. It caused Alicia and Apple to jerk apart with gasps of startlement.

Turning, Apple saw the source. The instrument was a walking stick handle. The one who had rapped it on the booth's glass side was an older man in a floppy hat.

Pulling the door open slightly, he accused them of not being in there to use the telephone, but to shelter from the rain or to pursue the rites of courtship.

"I wish neither to shelter nor spoon," he said. "I do wish to use the telephone."

Sheepishly they came out. As they were walking away, Alicia said, "When I'm with you I never know what's going to happen next." Which, Apple thought with a thrum of emotion, was one of the nicest things anyone had ever said to him.

They turned onto a main road. "What now?" Alicia asked. "I certainly don't want to go back and face all those reporters. They will have every entrance covered."

"We'll think about it while we eat."

"Yes, I still owe you a meal."

"We'll go to a restaurant."

"And then what do I do?"

Reluctantly, because he had to, Apple suggested, "There's my house, of course."

"The press might find us there," Alicia said. "It would not be hard for them to find out where you live."

"No, it wouldn't," Apple said. He wondered how Angus Watkin was going to feel about seeing his underling in the tabloids. Not too happy, Apple imagined, and worse if he found out that it was all a result of that obtuse idea about pickpockets.

"I have the answer," Alicia said. "Your country cottage.

We could go there. The reporters would not find it so easily as your city home, would they?"

"No, the cottage it is. Come on, let's get Ethel."

Because of the occult way that raindrops are able to make taxicabs disappear, except for people with coats and umbrellas, as well as cars of their own, Apple and Alicia, giving damp laughs at adversity, had to admit defeat and board a passing bus.

When they alighted the drizzle had let up. For spite, Apple waited until the sixth empty taxi came along in the following thirty seconds before raising his arm.

Soon they got out of the modern taxi by the old one. While being paid, the driver asked, "Is it for sale?" Apple said, "Not for all the gold in Threadneedle Street." Alicia patted his arm thoroughly.

And the exchange reminded him that Ethel was, indeed, distinctive, and that the press might know of, or be told of, her existence.

He therefore took quiet streets in heading cottagewards and chose a suburban restaurant which had a parking lot in the rear. From experience, he knew they hadn't been tailed.

Inside they sat at a corner table, satisfying Apple's spycraft fondness for such protection, but he played it down by sitting with his back to the room.

When Alicia returned from the washroom and from having telephoned Babushka, she said, "I have asked her to tell the reporters that I shall be showing up there anytime soon."

"Why'd you do that, Alicia?"

"Because that will keep them from nosing about elsewhere, you see."

"I do see," Apple said, smiling. "I see why you're a top world-class chess player."

"However, I did not say where we were going. Wild horses could not drag it out of Irini, naturally, but I know what telephone-receptionists are for listening in and then selling their information to newspapers."

"Yes, you're quite an expert at all this, aren't you?"

Nodding, Alicia reached across to give his hand a squeeze. "I cannot tell you how nice it is to be with someone like you, Jeff. Someone straightforward."

They smiled at one another lingeringly, Apple the while enjoying a secondary pleasure, that of feeling like a heel. It all helped keep his mind off his clammy bottom.

The waiter came. They ordered chicken soup and Dover sole with salad. That he had chosen well when he picked a medium-price white wine Apple could tell by the drabness in the waiter's eyes as he turned away.

When they were alone again, Alicia said, "And now, Jeff, what about the police?"

Apple stared at her blankly. "What about them? I don't know what about them."

"The kidnapping. Those criminals. Do we not have to report the affair to the pertinent authorities?"

"Ah yes," he said. "I see what you mean."

"You do not appear to be overly enthusiastic," Alicia said. "You do not have anything against the police, do you?"

"No no, nothing like that."

"If we leave it too late to report the matter, we might get into trouble."

"I doubt that, Alicia," Apple said. He was telling himself that being named and possibly pictured in the tabloids as the rumoured fiancé of a celebrity was bad enough, but being even innocently involved in what seemed to be a criminal act, plus having to attend identity parades and look at thousands of mug-shots in search of the snatchers —that wasn't acceptable, to either Upstairs or himself.

Alicia raised a forefinger. "As a foreigner, Jeff, I have to be careful."

Apple said, "You also have to be careful not to cause an international incident. Political inferences could easily be put on this business, which wouldn't bother me, but could be very awkward for you."

"Is that the reason for your lack of enthusiasm?"

"It is, yes. We should think it over before we do anything. As it stands now, the police know nothing."

"This is your country," Alicia said. "And as far as I am concerned, the less fuss the better."

Apple smiled. He said, "Anyway, I have the suspicion that those goons were a couple of amateurs."

"What gives you that impression?"

"Well, look how easily I dealt with them."

Dismissing that with the cough of scoff, Alicia said, "It was highly dangerous and you were magnificent." She went on to give a complete blow-by-miss account of the house scene, which lasted through most of the meal. Apple listened enthralled.

It had been a lively reunion in the farmyard, with Apple particularly pleased that Monico not only remembered Alicia but greeted her as an equal.

Now, Apple was about to usher them into Ethel when the farmhouse door opened. Galling appeared. Apple introduced him to Alicia, who, sparkling prettily from the wine, said what a wonderful warm evening it had turned out to be. "Do you not agree?"

Galling drew in a long breath, like someone considering an offer. Apple did the same, feeling a form of dread, regretting this impulse to stop and collect his dog, but he blurted the air out again when Galling said:

"You're right, miss. It is. In fact, we're having some beautiful weather just now."

Grateful for another good sign, Apple hustled Alicia and Monico into Ethel, with Farmer Galling bowing and smiling like a lecherous mandarin.

Seconds later they were at the cottage.

Inside, while Alicia went to the kitchen to make tea, Apple built a fire for the cheer of it. He had no idea what was going to happen next and he refused to allow himself to play with conjecture. He definitely did not think of making love by the firelight's glow.

When Alicia came in with cups, Apple made a smart turn to face the fire and hoped his backside would stop steaming at once. The tea they sipped standing together, with murmurs of appreciation. Monico stared like a taxidermist's masterwork at the paradise dogs find in flames.

"That is better," Alicia said, putting her cup on the mantelpiece. "And now we have to do something about our clothes." She gestured down at herself, as though showing off the black leather shortie coat, black wool sweater, white skirt and high white boots.

"Our clothes?"

"Yes, Jeff. Especially yours. I know that you are wetter than I am."

Apple mumbled that yes, he did seem to be a little damp. His thoughts were growing coy. Even so, he was startled when Alicia said, "All right, take them off."

"Take my clothes off?"

"So that I can put them by the fire to dry."

In one long trot Apple said, "That's an excellent idea you have there, Alicia, really it is."

She nodded. "Of course it is. Come along. Off with them." Holding out her hands, she twiddled the fingers.

Sniffing as though thinking about something else altogether, Apple moved away a pace or two to remove his jacket. As he reached it to Alicia—both stretching—he happened to glance down. Monico, he saw, was watching him with an old-fashioned look in his eyes.

Apple said, "I think I'll put the old fellow out to have a run about."

"Is he confined at the farm?"

Mumbling an affirmative lie, Apple took Monico across to the door and put him outside, receiving at the last second a look that wasn't so much old-fashioned as plain dirty.

Back near the hearth, soothed by the cozy lighting, Apple took off his shirt, which was perfectly dry. Airily, as though he did this sort of thing every Thursday, he tossed it to Alicia, who draped it beside his jacket on a chair.

Sitting on the couch, humming, Apple took off his shoes and socks. He was disappointed to note that his feet looked large and white and uninteresting. While putting his socks on again ("They're not a bit wet"), he said he would leave his shoes over here to dry out because leather should never be dried quickly. Oddments of information like that, he knew, were always appreciated.

"Fine," Alicia said. "Now your trousers."

"In fact, if your shoes get dried too quickly, it's not a bad thing to wet them again, and then give them a slow dry."

"I shall remember that always," Alicia said. "Your trousers, please."

Sniffing when not humming, and mumbling when not doing the airy act, Apple stood up and took off his slacks. He was a mite doubtful about the rabbits on his undershorts, but decided that they went to show—

What the rabbits went to show Apple never finished. As he tossed his slacks in Alicia's direction, two objects fell from the pockets and landed with sturdy plops on the rug. One was his home-made Alicia Suvov Fan Club badge, the other a wallet full of Jeff Poor documentation.

Apple gagged with worry.

It was instinct, not training, that made him move forwards and, legs spread, put a covering foot on each item, despite knowing that Alicia had already seen them. He said, "Ah so." He had no notion what it was supposed to mean.

"It is only the cuffs that are wet," Alicia said, holding the slacks up. "What have you dropped?"

"Things that belong to yesterday," Apple said, brilliantly, struck by the inspiration which sometimes came to him in his moments of profound need. It was as if his mind felt it owed him that much for the drawbacks of blushing, sentimentality and a romanticism to which he could find no cure.

Alicia turned her attention downwards. "What kind of yesterday things are they, Jeff?"

Stooping and scooping, Apple picked up the two items. He said, bravely not wincing at the pain as the badge's pin jabbed his palm, "This one is a lock of hair in fibreglass. The other is a wallet of photographs."

"Girl-friends?"

After nodding, Apple drew back his head to a semi-noble attitude to sling both items into the fire. For overdoing the head-angle and the dramatic swing of his arms, he forgave himself: a gallant gesture, he felt, even if untrue, called for a certain measure of stagecraft—and it all took the observer's mind farther away from suspicion. For this last sly thought, Apple forgave himself again.

In any case, he mused as he watched Alicia turn away with a demure and appreciative smile, if there really were pictures and momentoes involved, he might still have made the *beau geste*. She was worth it.

His worry of a second ago, Apple realised, when there was a chance of him being exposed as a phony, was for

Alicia more than for himself. He feared disappointing her as much as he feared losing her.

Trouser cuffs placed near the fire, Alicia went to the door. She returned with the trenchcoat that had been hanging on a peg there. "Here, Jeff. You must not catch a chill."

"It's quite muggy this evening, as a matter of fact," Apple said. "I feel warm."

"Then perhaps I shall put your coat on when I myself have undressed."

Apple mumbled at that, sniffed as Alicia eased him backwards to the couch, hummed until he had airily settled himself in a near-rakish sprawl.

Alicia had picked up Apple's discontinued humming. Although the tune was unrecognisable, in its character there seemed to be a hint of honky-tonk, albeit with a Russian flavour, like an upbeat "Volga Boatman."

Moving to the hum, Alicia removed her hip-length coat, which she threw onto a chair. She might have been alone for all the notice she took of the avid audience, her eyes sauntering everywhere except to the couch.

His ten toes scrunching together like elbowing yokels at a carnival, Apple watched without a single blink as the sweater came off and the head shook its hair back into shape. He would have applauded save for being inspired by the white-lace bra's valiant work of containment.

With a hand on the mantelpiece for balance, Alicia, still humming, heeled off her white boots. Somehow, avid audience didn't find the act all that stirring. Absently, he gave a forgiving smile.

He became still, toes included, when now Alicia began to ease down her skirt. She did so a languid inch or two at a time, in tune with short snatches of hum, the while swaying from side to side. Her hipswell passed, the skirt dropped to the floor.

Alicia stepped free. She turned slowly, like a fashion model, demonstrating her figure and the bra-matching panties that would have been small on a toddler.

Limp even to his toes, Apple stared blatantly at the inner wrists, the navel's wicked edge, both suggestive troughs under the shoulder-blades, the inside of the upper forearms and those arousing topswells of the calves. He smiled in gratitude.

Alicia gave back a smile of the same nature as, turn completed, she began to move towards the couch. Apple got up. Alicia came into his arms.

The kiss was short, sweet, prim, erotic. After it Alicia whispered, "Perhaps upstairs you will be kind enough to help me finish getting undressed."

In a post-lovemaking haze, his mind formed in a fat grin, Apple lay on the bed embracing Alicia. He loved the feel of her nakedness entangled with his own. That there was the danger of his left leg going to sleep he didn't care about; nor would he have cared at this juncture if the danger had been related to amputation.

However, it was in changing position, presently, to ease his leg but not reduce the quality of the embrace, that Apple came out of his haze to look at the realities.

He and Alicia had to go on together, he mused. That was certain. Which meant coming up with a particularly ingenious idea to keep Upstairs in the black-out. It would need a lot of serious thinking. It was sure to be an eight-slice problem, at least. And then what if Upstairs found out?

Apple decided to leave it there for the time being; to go hazewards and enjoy his contentment. He sighed.

Alicia, her head on his chest, murmured, "Are you feeling nice, Jeff?"

"No, I'm feeling wonderful, Alicia. And you?"

"Wanton and terrible and quite disgraceful. It's gorgeous."

"I'm so glad."

She raised her head. "Do you know what I would like now."

His mind's grin tweaked. "What?"

"A cigarette."

"Ah," he said. "Well, there's nothing like tradition."

"We did have a drink beforehand, even though it was only a cup of tea."

"I'll slip downstairs and get the cigs," Apple said, starting to disentangle himself.

Alicia said, "We'll both go. I'll race you."

As fast as three blinks she was out of his arms and bounding off the bed. Apple, naked except for his socks, leapt up and gave chase. He felt as gleeful as a schoolboy.

Downstairs, with them both panting and chortling, Apple got cigarettes and lit two. After taking one, Alicia helped him into his trenchcoat, tying the belt, fussing like a mum. As she turned, heading for the kitchen with a remark about putting the kettle on, Apple nodded to himself that he would get her undies from the bedroom. He put his cigarette in an ashtray, went to the stairs and lightly up.

Over the bedroom threshold Apple jerked to a halt. His mouth made a strange shape. He stared in disbelief and outrage and a kind of melancholy at the open window.

Half-way through it was a man, leaving. He was young, blond, fresh-faced and with an upturned nose. He wore jeans and a dark sweater. He was holding a video camera.

Appearing by his expression to be torn between amusement and worry, the snub-nosed blond, who had paused at Apple's entrance, started to push on out from his sitting position straddling the sill.

With a snarl for Angus Watkin, for how devilishly he had won in the end, having had the sex filmed from inside the clothes closet, Apple sprang forwards. He reached the window in three long strides. With both hands he made a grab. He said nothing because the bedroom door was open and his voice might carry downstairs.

That this spelled the finish as far as he and Alicia were concerned, Apple was trying to ignore. If he could get the film back, if he could keep Alicia from knowing about the filming . . .

He and the man performed an untidy slap-and-grapple, until Apple realised that it wasn't the man he wanted, to hold or hurt, but the evidence. He grabbed the camera.

Between him and Snub-nose there was a brief, silent tugging back and forth. Then, snappingly, Apple won.

With the camera in his hands he went stumbling backwards. The backs of his legs hit the bed and he fell over. Impetus rolled him across to the other side and down onto the rug, where he sat up.

He looked fast at the window. Snub-nose had gone—it was a manageable drop to the lawn. Quickly, Apple wrenched at the camera's loading lid. It flipped up. The space inside was empty. The man had already removed the cassette.

Apple sprang to his feet like a dancing savage. The camera he dropped on the bed before leaping to within reach of the door, which with a wide-swinging arm he slapped to send it into its frame. He went to the window.

Having been through this routine often before, for exercise and entertainment, Apple was able to be swift about getting through the window space to an outside sit. From there he pushed down into a headlong dive.

He landed correctly, on his hands, and then gave two complete rolls, arriving against the shoulder-high hedge which separated garden from road.

He jumped up. The scene was amply illuminated by a glow of light coming through the parlour curtains.

Nearby lay Snub-nose, on his back. Standing on top of him was Monico, teeth gleaming. He wanted to play, though this couldn't be known by the blond.

Apple was about to take a deep, settling breath when Snub-nose brought something from under his sweater. There was a metallic glint. Apple gasped. Despite knowing that Alicia would be bound to hear, he was about to yell not to shoot, when the man flung the object away. It wasn't a gun, Apple saw as it sailed over the hedge, but the cassette.

He threw his upper body onto the hedge's metre-broad top. The twigs of privet jabbed at him through his trenchcoat and the neatly clipped structure swayed madly forwards; but Apple saw the cassette's destination.

The man who caught it between clapped hands was of average build and, like his colleague, wearing jeans and a sweater. He had a hard, hawk face under a crew cut. Behind him stood a van with IDEAL BAKERY written on the side.

The man was turning towards the vehicle as the hedge, its forward surge completed, twanged the other way. Apple was tossed back onto the lawn.

While he was recovering his balance, having managed to stay upright, he heard the van's motor start with a roar. His hesitation was short. He ran past where Snub-nose was still being pinned by the grinning Monico and reached the side patch of gravel.

As he did, he glimpsed the van's tail-lights whisk away. Next, he twitched with surprise as a car suddenly appeared, going in the same direction. A big black Humber, it sped silently after the bread van.

Then, from out of a gap in the hedge opposite, a motor-cycle shot into view. Its helmeted rider went off in pursuit of the Humber.

Apple, standing beside Ethel, was still blinking about that when another engine noise turned his head. Along came an open MG sports car. The driver, a man in a low-pulled cap, sat crouched over the wheel as he careened past after the others.

So, Apple thought, at least three of the Dwarfs were still in the running. As though things weren't bad enough without competition. But the game wasn't over yet.

Rippling swiftly into Ethel, Apple got his emergency key from under the rubber mat, jabbed it home and pressed the starter.

So what would Alicia do? Apple wondered as, having reversed off the gravel, he ripped away after the other vehicles. He was wondering thus to keep himself from judging the chase situation logically, realising that it was hopeless and giving up.

Ethel sped around a bend in the hedge-sided lane, which was only just two-cars wide. Her headlights ripped open a vast wedge in the total, country darkness. There was no sign of other lights ahead.

Alicia, Apple mused on in answering his question, would see his cigarette smouldering in the ashtray and from that conclude that his absence was momentary. She would think he had gone outside for something or up to the bathroom. She would finish preparing the tea. She would wait. She would drink her own tea and wait some more. When he didn't show up after a reasonable length of time, she would probably investigate.

Ethel came onto a straight section of road, of which there were few thereabouts. The stretch was a quarter-mile long. It was bare of traffic.

Alicia would go outside, Apple thought implacably. She

would see that her boy-friend had not taken his dog for a walk because the dog was there—Snub-nose, soon realising that Monico was harmless, would have pushed him off and left, no doubt to call in his gloat to Angus Watkin that the caper was a hit: Icy Alice had been filmed in sexual congress and could now be made to dance to an Upstairs tune.

Scanning the darkness ahead, Apple questioned nervously if the other drivers could have turned off somewhere. But there hadn't been a side road yet, he reminded himself. Unless they had gone into a field.

Apple lowered his foot still more on the accelerator, musing on: Back inside the cottage, with nowhere downstairs left to check, Alicia might go upstairs. Bathroom and guest quarters seen to be empty, she would certainly look in the main bedroom. That would be the end of her search and the end of everything. She would see the camera.

Ethel swept into a curve, leaving the straight stretch behind. Apple's nerves yammered like lunatics under the full moon as a pair of headlights smacked into view, coming this way, which ended his groan that he hadn't had the sense to hide the camera. The approaching vehicle went by at an uncomfortably close range and Ethel was back facing an empty road.

Alicia, Apple tried telling himself, did not necessarily have to jump to the conclusion that the camera had just been used for filming their lovemaking. His try didn't work. The scene was too peculiar, she herself too wised up and suspicious.

Apple went back to groaning. This time it was while he pictured Alicia's face. He saw the slow change of expression from amused puzzlement at his absence to deep hurt as the camera gave her what seemed to be the sick truth:

the man she had put her trust in had, after all, turned out to be just another conniver, a phony, a cheat.

Ethel came to a fork in the road. Apple slowed, hesitated, thought to go left and then to go right and last of all stopped altogether.

This is a terrible waste of time, he fumed, his hands and feet dithering at the controls like some rhythmless someone trying to beat time to a tune he disliked in the first place. Choose, you idiot.

If I were the odious Wily Watkin, Apple thought, which fork would I take? Well, the right one, because people, expecting the devious, would assume I'd gone left. But then, if they knew I was devious . . .

Giving up, Apple took the direction that was fractionally closer, being on his own side of the road. He picked up speed as fast as he could run the gears through.

With Alicia it wouldn't be that way in any case, Apple mused dully. She, assuming her lover's absence to be quite normal, due to something mundane, would placidly drink her tea and doze off in front of the fire. Not for anything would she even consider poking around in other people's cottages.

Ahead lay a hill. As Apple saw it, the crest was flicked by lights. They were followed by three other sets, the last recognisable as belonging to the MG.

And, Apple thought triumphantly, perking, while Alicia sat dozing by the fire, her trusty lover would be recovering the evidence. This he could do on account of the advantages he had going for him:

He wasn't barefoot, for he had cleverly, presciently put his socks on again. He wasn't entirely naked, because, shrewdly, he had thought to don his trenchcoat. These lanes he knew like the back of his hand, whereas the others were strangers here. And while to them this endeavour was little more than a game, a lightweight caper, to him it was a matter of love and war, one which he was determined to win, if only on account of that expression of hurt on Alicia's face.

Ethel shot valiantly up the hill.

Apple swayed his torso forwards and back to help things along. If ever he had been glad of the money he had spent on specialists to keep Ethel in perfect health, as it related to her age, it was now.

She reached the brow of the hill, went over. On the downslope below, the four sets of lights could be seen: the sports car's, the motor-cycle's, the Humber's, the bread van's. They were running close.

The last three had to be removed or put behind before he could get a chance at what their drivers also wanted, the cassette, Apple thought with false cheer. He declined to see the task as impossible, just as he was refusing to admit that he felt insecure minus his underpants, or that if he did get hot-golden lucky and recovered that cassette it would probably mean the end of his career.

Apple didn't reduce speed as Ethel went down the hill. He knew that what at the bottom appeared to be a dangerous bend was only a topographical illusion. But the others wouldn't know. It would cause them to slow.

He could see them doing exactly that as, spaced by some thirty metres, they took the bend one at a time and went from sight. When the MG came into view again, seconds later, Ethel rounding the same curve, the sports car was close enough to be in the headlights' full blast.

There were more bends. Knowing them all, Apple maintained his pace, shrinking the gap like a greyhound after whippets. The open MG's driver repeatedly threw fast glances back. To kill the undipped, relentless headlight glare from Ethel, he took off his cap and hung it on the rear-view mirror.

There was another straight stretch. Apple saw that the way he was closing in on the sports car was making it gain on the motor-cycle, which was therefore being forced to get nearer to the Humber, which was having to creep up on the bread van.

The five were evenly and closely spaced as they curved off the straight and roared past a cottage, where two children, evidently thinking that the procession was a rally, waved with encouraging cheers. Sparing a hand from his tricky top-speed driving, Apple automatically waved back.

Ethel, trembling grimly, came to within two metres of the open sports car. As everything he had ever learned relating to a situation like this had gone from his mind, Apple simply charged on, drawing out to pass.

Predictably, the sports car also moved out of line, barring the way. And when Ethel switched back, the other car did the same. There was now less than a metre between the two, and they were travelling at sixty miles an hour.

At the same speed but with a slightly safer gap between went the other vehicles. The motor-cycle similarly swept from side to side in preventing the passing of the MG while itself trying to safely pass the Humber, which tacked across the road to stop that as well as aim to overtake the leader, whose zig-zagging was forestalling that act.

A village appeared. Like five vehicles in search of a sober driver, the bread van, Humber, motor-bike, MG and Ethel sped weavingly along the one main street. A man who was leaving a pub went back in again.

Beyond the last house lay a traffic roundabout, starkly lit from high above. Until the five arrived, it was deserted. By the time Apple got there, he had planned his move.

The sports car, like the others, turned onto the circle in the legitimate direction. Ethel swiftly went the other way.

Her high body on a slant, she careened at full steam around to the far side, where the bread van had branched off, and which she reached at the same time as the sports car.

She and it left the roundabout neck and neck. The uncapped driver, face familiar from Viscount Tower's lobby, slapped his cap on again with a gesture of determination and swooped into a hunch over the steering-wheel.

It looked as though he were going to pour on speed, of which his mount had much more than Apple's. But there was nowhere for him to go unless he ran over the motorcyclist, who couldn't get out of the way because of the big Humber, which couldn't . . .

The rally went into a long curve, with Ethel and the MG still abreast. The curve was to Apple's advantage, being on his side of the road. Having visualised the byways ahead, he realised that this was probably his best chance. He faced it with his chin out.

Accepting that if a car came along now the result would be almost certainly fatal, Apple put his foot down. He gave Ethel her freedom. As any woman would, she took it like a shot. Her carburetor gate open wide, she fled as wildly as a wanton around the bend and into danger.

The sports car, disadvantaged further by being on the outer rim, began to edge back. Its driver and Apple exchanged frequent glances. By his expression, the Dwarf was both annoyed at being overtaken and impressed with Apple's stupidity.

When the radiator of the MG was nearing Ethel's middle, its driver gave in. By taking off his cap and then throwing it away, he signalled, *You win, you crazy bastard.* The sports car slid behind.

Rarely in his life had Apple been more flattered. For one and a half seconds, he forgot Alicia. He floated off and looked at himself. Here he was, in Ethel, speeding through the night on a mission and getting respect from professional, foreign espionage agents.

Snapping back, putting his goody away for another time, and many of them, Apple steered over to the legal side of the road. That an oncoming vehicle didn't appear at once was a faint disappointment, but Apple had learned to be philosophical in the spy business.

The road straightened out. Directly ahead was the helmeted motor-cyclist. Apple owned one sure way of putting him out of the running. All you had to do with a car was touch, not even hit, the rear, and the machine was lost, as out of control as a plane without a tail.

Apple, however, knew with no pause for consideration that he couldn't bring himself to do that. The bike would crash, the man would be injured if not killed, and at these speeds it was more likely to be the latter.

But, Apple reminded himself, the cyclist didn't know of his pursuer's unfortunate lack of ruthlessness. Better still, Apple realised, he didn't even know he was an agent, thought him a nuisance called Jeff Poor, a nuisance definitely not to be trusted.

Meaning, whereas all spies had roughly the same training and therefore could be relied on to act in the same cautious way in the same situation, to not rock the boat, your innocent outsider would barge in with no notion of the havoc and crises he could create.

Maybe the motor-cyclist was expecting the worst, Apple mused, noting contiguously that there did seem to be a hint of panic in the way the bike was swooshing back and forth in its attempts to get past the Humber. So how about a little dose of stage dressing?

Urged, Ethel bowled forwards. As the clutch and gas pedal were toyed with, she began to emote like a female baritone. She was at full, noisy throttle by the time she arrived immediately behind the bike.

Its rider threw a look back. Beyond the helmet's plastic visor his eyes were mostly whites. He switched his machine across the road and back while keeping his front wheel no more than a metre from the Humber, which space was twice the distance between his back wheel and Ethel, who ranted on with the aria as her clutch was ridden.

Nervous that he might make a mistake, actually hit the motor-bike, Apple dropped back. But he decided on one more try, using everything he could muster in the way of noise to create psychological damage.

When he roared forwards again, Apple had the radio on at a full blast of static, was pressing the horn and, with his head out of the window, was screaming a war-cry at the top of his vocal range.

For a fraction of a second, the motor-cyclist let go of the handlebars in a dither of shock. He also rose perceptibly from the saddle. Back in contact again, he swerved at a sharp angle into the side of the road.

Apple had passed almost before he knew it had happened. Withdrawing his head, releasing the horn and breathing again after that scream, he switched off the radio and allowed himself a pause for relieved relaxation.

It was a short pause. Apple knew he mustn't delay. If the bread van got into traffic and London-bound, all would most likely be lost. He had to make his strike of retrievement in the byways, if possible.

But Apple was forced to acknowledge that, if a motorcycle couldn't get by the Humber here, there wasn't much hope for Ethel—short of another convenient roundabout.

Again Apple visualised the road ahead. There were no traffic circles. There was nothing other than winding lanes for the next two or three miles.

Apple did, however, remember that last year when

there had been a road-blocking accident, traffic had been rerouted along tracks that served smallholdings. It was, in fact, a short cut, though the surface was fit for nothing more sophisticated than a tractor.

Even while remembering, Apple made up his mind. So what he had to do now was see if he could recognise the landmark, a barn, which indicated where the off-turning lay.

That, in the event, was no problem. A minute later the whitewashed barn showed up at a distance in the bread van's headlights like a sheet to a lantern. When the van had gone by, it was the Humber's turn to play flop slideshow. Next came Ethel.

Apple saw the off-turning, opposite the barn. With the hope of fooling those who were coming along in the rear, he made his departure from the road a thing of awkward-ness, suddenly cutting off with a shriek of tyre-rubber as though all this weren't planned but accidental.

Ethel came onto a mud track. With the motor-cycle and the sports car flashing past behind on the road, she hit a bump and rose gracefully in the air.

Her landing had less grace. The old leaf-type springs did their best, but the thud of the squat still shook every nut and bolt and rivet and hinge.

With a cough of apology to Ethel, Apple recovered from his own battering. There would, he knew, be more of the same, recalling the grotty track over which he and other traffic had travelled as cautiously as nudists through barbed wire. But caution meant rickling along, and the situation yelled out for haste.

Coughing after every few breaths, Apple kept up his speed as he steered along the track. Mainly it was straight. On either side lay neat springtime crops and their wild relations. Ethel leapt over bumps, bucked and reared, crashed in and out of ruts, splashed through pools of rain-water.

To divert himself from the punishment to Ethel, Apple considered his move if he should fail to recover the cassette from the bread van driver.

Whether Alicia had found the camera or not wouldn't be relevant, he mused. He would still have to tell her about it when he got back to the cottage, because in time she would know. Sooner or later she would be approached by one of Angus Watkin's people, shown the film, threatened with its release if she didn't do what Upstairs wanted.

Yes, Apple thought, he would tell Alicia the truth about himself. He would blow his cover, explain what the caper had been for and try to make her believe that the filming had been done without his knowledge.

Was it believable?

Aware of the answer, Apple put on speed and went into a steady coughing. The cassette had to be recovered—and in any manner at all. You couldn't fight foul with fair.

Some of those apologetic coughs were for Apple himself, his sensibilities, though he neither knew it nor cared to know it. That he was in an unredeemingly dirty profession he understood only on an obscure level of consciousness, the same place wherein he suspected himself of owning decency and grace. Such attributes could only be a beneficial addition to the trade, he would have reasoned had he been crude enough to plumb so far into self-intimacy. Instead, avoiding debate on why precisely he was a spy, he clouded it all by holding implacably to his romantic view of the gangrenous/fatuous world of espionage.

Squeaking and clanking, throwing up sprays of puddle-water, Ethel went on. Between patches of flatness she performed her graceful leaps and crunchy landings. Apple's throat grew raspy from his coughing. He was oozingly glad to see the pair of massive elm trees that formed the detour's end.

And at almost that same moment he saw the lights. Four flashes were coming and going through a thick hedge over to his left. The first seemed to be about the same distance from the elms as Ethel.

Who now leapt forwards in response to Apple's request —his foot going flat to the floor. She flinched and skittered like a horse under fire, but she kept on course. It was as though she knew they had to reach the elms before the bread van.

With one last, mammoth leap Ethel left the track behind. At an arc she careened between the huge trees—and into a side-on blast of headlights. The bread van was right there.

While Ethel was straightening at a wobble from her turn onto the road, the van came alongside. Apple caught a glimpse of its driver, a man with the face of a weasel under his crew cut. He sat stern at the wheel, like a helmsman in a vicious storm, even though Ethel was being beaten.

This time the curve was to the opposition's benefit. But Weasel also had the risk of being on the wrong side of the road. He grew gradually ahead in his far younger vehicle and Apple wondered in his desperation if he should try ramming.

A car appeared, approaching. Instinctively Apple braked. The bread van shot ahead and cut in sharply. There was a loud clang in time with a jerk at Ethel's front. She had been struck.

The car passed, the van sped on.

Apple followed with his heart settling from the jig-beat it had gone into when Ethel had received her hit. Insisting to himself that, as she was performing well, the blow could only have been superficial, he patted the dashboard. That he had considered ramming he forgot.

The bread van went on, chased at a reckless pace by Ethel, the Humber, the motor-cycle and the sports car. The road topped a rise, straightening as it did. Beyond was a long downhill stretch, with spread out prettily at the bottom the lights of a small town.

Apple nodded encouragement to himself in respect of East Wither. Its main street was usually crowded with traffic. Jams and double-parking were as common as colds in March.

Should Weasel get stopped in his bread van, or merely delayed momentarily, Apple planned, that would be the time to dismount and strike.

Praying for East Wither to have the traffic congestion of its life, Apple sent Ethel rolling down the hill. She, like everyone else in the rally, swooped from side to side.

The first, outlying houses began to flash by. Cars came past. Pedestrians appeared as well as street-lamps. The bread van had to slow to get around a man wobbling about on a pedal-bicycle. Apple tensed himself for action on foot.

He was unnerved by the shriek. Next he was delighted. Next he began to worry.

The train whistle shrieked again. It was followed by the clang of a bell near at hand. Apple had forgotten about the railway crossing here.

Beyond the van he could see the gates with their flashing red light starting to move, to close the road. He also saw, however, that Weasel might just get there in time to cross, leaving all his pursuers behind.

Apple would have driven right up to the van except for another pedal-bike getting in the way. It wasn't the only one. Two girls on bikes slipped out into the road smack in front of the bread van. It came to a fast halt.

Apple was already steering Ethel up the kerb as Weasel got out. The agent left the van where it stood and ran towards the near-closed gate.

Stopping half on the pavement, switching off, Apple flung himself out of Ethel and spent no more than two seconds examining the front damage (bent bumper) before racing after Weasel, who had just slipped through the closing barrier's last offering of gap.

Ignoring the smaller, pedestrian gate at the side, Apple ran straight at the five-foot-tall barrier. He didn't want to risk being cut off by the nearing train, giving Weasel the half-minute he needed to lose himself.

Apple had a fast look back. He saw the Humber, the motor-bike and the sports car being quickly and haphazardly abandoned. Several passers-by had stopped to watch.

Slapping both hands onto the gate's top bar, Apple threw his body up sideways. It was a stylish vault. All would have been well if, A, there hadn't been a stream of people crossing the railway lines towards him and, B, he had been wearing something under his trenchcoat.

Which garment, as he began his smooth downfloat, billowed up around him like a parachute; even, in that resemblance, seeming to slow down the descent, to Apple's further chagrin.

Of the nearby, lines-crossing women, Apple's fast glance showed, one opened her mouth in disbelief while another two pointed in horror. All the men but one sniggered. That one, older and bowler-hatted, gave a gasp of outrage.

Apple landed. He landed badly, being distracted, and having half his mind struggling under a collapsed tent in the Sahara. But he became fully alert, dismissing both his anatomical display and his threatening blush, when he realised that Weasel was slipping through the pedestrian gate at the far side.

His knee ached from the twisty landing and his stock-inged feet hurt from the oversized gravel of the railway bed, yet Apple pushed off from his recovery lean on the barrier to give chase. He covered only one metre.

The older man had suddenly got in his way, with be-hind him two of the women. All three bore the tremble of indignation. All were breathing heavily. All were snap-ping out remarks about public disgraces, and people like animals, and fetching coppers, and sex maniacs that ought to be behind bars.

The man clutched the trenchcoat belt. He appeared to be so feeble that a nudge would send him flying, but he held on tight as Apple tried to get away.

Giving his bowler hat a masterful tap on top, the old man panted, "Fetch a copper." One of the women said, "Flogging's too good for suchlike." The other said she wouldn't be surprised if he did it again, any minute now. She resettled her glasses.

Afraid of hurting the old man, Apple launched into an impassioned claim that it was all a terrible misunderstand-ing. As he did, the rest of the rally drivers went by, one man after the other, each scrambling over the barrier and hustling past.

The whistle shrieked.

To hear better against the train's growing thunder, the indignant trio leaned close to Apple, who raised his voice in explaining about the impromptu steeplechase which he and some of the other lads from the police training college had organised in the changing room after rugby practice but all on the spur of the moment so that a few of them were wearing only their hats and they should be coming along anytime now.

The old man let go with a distantly poignant smile, the women bustled off to the pedestrian gate and Apple decided, for reasons of fear, not to take a chance on jumping across lines in front of the now-booming train.

He was about to walk back and forth to aid his impatience when he saw there was no need: the passing train was merely an engine without carriages. And he was about to slip around behind it when he realised that possibly Weasel had pulled an old but effective trick.

In a situation like this, outnumbered, you didn't take the object of desire or contention with you—you left it behind. After drawing off pursuers you slipped back. You would run evasive action far better, think far better, because of the fact that it wouldn't be fatal (being minus the object) if you were caught: desperate men give less than perfect performances.

Apple turned with a salute to the old man, swung onto and over the gate, landed discreetly with knees together, ran past where the two women waited under a lamp-post and arrived at the bread van.

Pulling the door open, Apple leaned inside. He scuffled on a dashboard shelf, he poked into pockets on both doors, he felt under the seat.

His hand touched something warm, whereas all else was chill. The something's warmth came from body contact; from being in Weasel's pocket.

His eyes lush, hardly able to credit the luck, Apple put the cassette in a pocket of the trenchcoat as he backed out. He opened up the van's front and swiftly disabled the engine by removing the distributor's rotor-arm. As he threw it away, he saw Weasel. He was on his way back, dodging around the just-opening gate and with none of the others in view behind.

Apple raced to Ethel, slammed inside. He started the motor and reversed, making a crescent towards the railway crossing. Narrowly, he missed hitting Weasel, who then leapt up onto Ethel's rear. He stood on the bumper and held onto the roof-rack.

Since it could prove lethal to a person if you shook him off a moving car, but mostly because the necessary snap-swerves would be bad for Ethel's steering gear, Apple stopped and quickly got out. Around at the back he grabbed Weasel by the neck and the seat of his jeans, jerked him free of his hold and, swinging away, threw him mightily over the front of a parked car. Landing messily, Weasel let out a string of curses. Apple was shocked.

It had been a fast ride. He swung onto the gravel and brought Ethel to a hard stop. Killing lights and engine, he got out. He stood to listen. Apart from the motor's tickings and settlings, there was silence.

Quietly Apple circled behind Ethel towards the cottage. The parlour window was curtained and lit as before. Above, the bedroom window hadn't been closed. There was no sign of Monico anywhere.

Patting the pockets of his trenchcoat tensely, Apple went to the door. He softly turned the handle, softly pushed the door in, softly entered.

He said, "Well, hello."

"Hello," Alicia said. Her voice was different. Face bland in the soft lighting, she sat on the couch opposite the hearth. She was fully dressed. Monico lay sprawled at her feet.

Apple closed the door behind him. "You must've wondered what the hell had become of me."

"Yes, I did."

"So you investigated."

"Naturally," Alicia said, calm. "I was worried."

Apple asked, "You went upstairs? The master bedroom?"

"Of course."

"And, of course, you found the camera."

Alicia gave a single deep nod. "That is right."

Apple came forwards from the threshold, causing Monico to thump the rug twice with his tail by way of greeting. Apple stood with his back to the fire.

"You're not going to like this, Alicia," he said. "I mean, I know you don't like it already, because you must've been putting all kinds of interpretations on it. But I imagine it's worse than you've guessed."

"I do not understand."

By necessity playing the innocent, Apple said, "It's not a press job."

"I see."

"That's what I thought when I caught that man upstairs in the act of splitting. I thought he was a press photographer. I got the video camera from him but he'd already taken out the cassette."

Alicia stated, "You chased him."

Apple nodded. Not mentioning the Dwarfs, he went on to relate laconically how he had followed and finally caught up to this bread van.

"And then I got a shock," he ended. "When I threw that sly-looking character off Ethel, he let rip with a few choice swear words. The language he used was Russian."

"I see. Yes, quite a shock."

"He has to be KGB, I suppose."

"I suppose."

Apple said, "So it looks as though this filming job was to bring you into line."

Shrugging one shoulder, Alicia said, "But you did get the cassette back."

"Yes, I did."

"I thought you might. That was why I waited. Give it to me, please."

"I'm going to destroy it. Honestly."

"Please give me the cassette," Alicia said firmly.

Apple held out flat hands. "You don't think, do you, that I had anything to do with this?"

"No, I do not."

"Really?"

"Absolutely."

"And surely, Alicia, you don't still think I'm some kind of a spy, do you?"

Alicia shook her head. She now had a faint smile. "No, Jeff. You checked out. You failed the tests. The motor-cycle ride. Before that, the dog."

"What dog?"

"The one that attacked you outside Viscount Tower. An agent would have dealt with it easily."

"Ah," Apple said. "Yes. You were responsible for the dog."

"We were," Alicia said. She brought the gun out of her pocket with a slow movement. Monico raised his head, saw the automatic, settled down again to his doze. From her lap Alicia aimed at Apple, who asked, "Is that thing real?" He had already started to feel sad.

"As real as I am, Jeff."

"And is it loaded?"

"With six bullets."

"Would you use it?"

"On you, Jeff?" Alicia said. "Probably not. But guns are very dangerous. Do you not agree?"

"I certainly do. I don't like guns."

"Good. Then please give me the cassette."

"This isn't necessary," Apple said, kidding himself. "I'll be more than happy to destroy it for you." He brought out the black oblong.

"Destroy what has taken me days to create?" Alicia asked. Her smile grew a tinge warmer.

Apple nodded, slowly to match his sadness. He said, "You set it up when you telephoned during dinner."

"Yes, Jeff."

"You couldn't do it the first time you called Irini, because I was with you, in the phone box."

"No, Jeff. Dear Irini is never involved. She is too sweet and simple. I adore her."

"So other people arranged this?"

"Yes."

Apple knew now that the phony snatch wasn't Angus Watkin's work. It could only have been a KGB job, to make Alicia's willingness to be bedded believable. But he didn't say so because that would make him seem too wise, too much the spook, and he was trying not to believe any of this anyway.

But he did ask, "Is Viscount Tower really full of newspaper reporters?"

"No, Jeff. I told you that so we would have an acceptable reason for going somewhere together."

"Very clever," Apple said. He was sad.

"The cassette, please."

"Shall I put it on the floor and slide it across to you with my foot? That's what they do in the movies." He warned himself: don't get bitter.

"Nothing so drab," Alicia said. "Please throw it to me. I enjoy the risk."

Lightly, Apple tossed the cassette across. Alicia grabbed it out of the air like an expert and put it inside her coat. She said, "And, by the by, talking of enjoyment, I have thoroughly enjoyed the interlude with you, Jeff." She smiled. "All of it."

Stonily: "Thank you."

"I think you are charming and I do not want you to dislike me. I do not want you to think badly of me."

"How do people usually think of Russian spies?"

"I am not a spy, Jeff. I have never been a KGB agent."

"Can that be true?"

"It is," Alicia said pleasantly. "I do what I do for a variety of reasons. Perhaps one of them is that the KGB have evidence against me, or mine, and I have to do what they want. Perhaps not. It does not really matter. I have no complaints."

"Yes, you've done all this before, of course," Apple said. He had a slapdash try at putting on a sophisticated facade, gave up and sighed. Apple was sad.

"And with success," Alicia said. "I was all set to snare an Israeli agent, calling himself Edward Baker, but he didn't show up."

Apple awarded himself several points for saving Baker, but felt no better. He could see how Alicia would be valuable to the KGB, snaring people who, in time, could be pressured into usefulness.

"I was glad he did not appear, that Baker," Alicia said. "It allowed me to concentrate on you."

"But what is anyone going to do with a film of a harmless philologist?"

"No one is entirely harmless, Jeff. I dare say a busdriver could be made use of, if only on one single occasion."

"I suppose that's true."

"Your case, however, is not so low on the scale," Alicia said. "Recently you were at a conference in Paris, I am told. It was for the Intelligence services of the Common Market countries. You were the main interpreter, and you stayed in room one twenty-seven at the King George Hotel."

Apple nodded. "Right." He felt like an amateur.

"Chances are you will have interesting things to recount of that, also of others that you will no doubt attend in the future. You are not a star catch, Jeff, admittedly, but not too bad."

"And if I decline to play?"

Alicia patted the cassette through her coat. "Sooner or later, sometime, perhaps now, there will be someone whom you do not wish to see this film."

Apple shrugged. "You may be right. I suppose you're referring to love."

"I dare say I am. Is there anything more important?"

"No."

"For instance, I love my life, the style of it, the flow of it. I would do anything to protect that. Would you not?"

"No idea."

"And if I have to do things like seducing charming, tall and attractive men, then I have to bear it." She smiled. "But now I must go."

"On foot?"

After leaning down to give Monico a pat, Alicia rose. She held the gun casually, knowingly. "The cameraman is waiting in a car along the road," she said. "He has already taken his camera back." She began to move semi-sideways towards the door.

The situation, Apple felt, called for some statement, a pronouncement of import, substance, profundity. He could think of nothing. That made him sadder.

Alicia drew the door open. With her free hand she blew a kiss. "Good-bye, Jeff."

"Good-bye, Alicia."

"Thank you for a wonderful few days," she said. With a last smile she went out and closed the door.

Apple turned, leaned on the mantelpiece and looked down into the sad flames.

EPILOGUE

After a moment Apple roused himself. He went to the door and locked it securely. Back at the hearth he brought out of his other trenchcoat pocket a cassette. It was the first one, the one of himself and Alicia making love upstairs, filmed by Snub-nose.

On hearing Weasel speak Russian, realising the job was a KGB, not a Watkin, Apple had decided to be prepared. He had taken from Ethel's glove compartment one of last week's video movies. He hoped to palm it off onto Snub-nose, if he should still be around the cottage and dangerous. In the event, Alicia had taken it.

Apple looked at the cassette. Although the film couldn't be used to pressure Alicia with maximum effect, it was still worth a lot to Angus Watkin, personally, for he would let rivals know he had succeeded where they had failed. Which meant that it was worth a lot to the underling. It could turn him into an upperling, or at least start him off in that direction.

Apple sighed. With no grandness in his gesture, he tossed the cassette into the fire. Watching the plastic begin to warp and sizzle, he hoped that Alicia and the KGB would enjoy seeing *Seance on a Wet Afternoon.*

About the author

Marc Lovell is the author of nine previous Appleton Porter novels, including *The Spy Who Barked in the Night* and *The Spy Who Got His Feet Wet*. *Apple Spy in the Sky* was made into the film *Trouble at the Royal Rose*. Mr. Lovell has lived for over twenty years on the island of Majorca.